"Why am I here?"

"Every small town needs a good-looking cowboy." Jackie grinned. "Plus, you're famous to boot. I'm sure the tourists would love to meet a real bull rider."

Max's jaw tightened. "Yeah, that was my father's thought, too." The man had ignored him until he started making a name in the PBR circuit. All of a sudden, Max was good for business.

He stuffed his hands into his pockets. "I'm going. Tomas needs to rest, and we still have a bunch of stuff to do at the ranch." He turned to leave.

"Max." She caught up with him before he made it outside. "I was just teasing. I didn't mean to upset you. Most people don't mind being called good-looking."

He saw concern in her eyes. Riding bulls was so much easier than dealing with life.

He feared she saw the weakness in him.

The truth of who he was.

A seventh-generation Texan, **Jolene Navarro** fills her life with family, faith and life's beautiful messiness. She knows that as much as the world changes, people stay the same: vow-keepers and heartbreakers. Jolene married a vow-keeper who shows her holding hands never gets old. When not writing, Jolene teaches art to inner-city teens and hangs out with her own four almost-grown kids. Find Jolene on Facebook or her blog, jolenenavarrowriter.com.

Books by Jolene Navarro

Love Inspired

Lone Star Legacy

Texas Daddy
The Texan's Twins
Lone Star Christmas

Lone Star Holiday
Lone Star Hero
A Texas Christmas Wish
The Soldier's Surprise Family

Love Inspired Historical

Lone Star Bride

Lone Star Christmas

Jolene Navarro

Recycling programs
for this product may
not exist in your area.

LOVE INSPIRED BOOKS

ISBN-13: 978-1-335-50986-4

Lone Star Christmas

Copyright © 2018 by Jolene Navarro

www.Harlequin.com

Printed in U.S.A.

Trust in the Lord with all thine heart;
and lean not unto thine own understanding.
In all thy ways acknowledge him,
and he shall direct thy paths.
—*Proverbs* 3:5–6

In memory of my mother-in-law,
Francisca Guerrero Navarro.
Te amo con todo mi corazón.

Chapter One

Bitter winds whipped through the valley and down the back of Max Delgado's neck. Twenty years had passed since his last visit to the ranch. The Delgado Ranch, his family's homestead since the early 1800s. He carried the name of the first Delgado in Texas: Maximiliano Francisco Puentes Delgado. Always sounded a bit pretentious to him.

Looking over the fence to the vast landscape, he tried to pull up memories of his childhood, but being here didn't help. He had been told he'd spent most of his early years here with his mother. There was probably a reason they were so elusive, or maybe he just didn't have a good memory. He tended to live in the moment. It was easy, and he liked easy.

His focus went back to the broken gate. November was never this cold in the Texas Hill Country. The way his life had been going the last few months, though, he probably shouldn't be surprised.

Right on cue, the rotten wood crumbled in his gloved hand, the old hardware now useless. The corral was in worse shape than Max had first thought. He'd need a truckload of panels before he put any bulls in this pen.

He had hauled a couple practice bulls along with his favorite horses.

They were getting restless and needed to be unloaded. He glanced back at the neglected pens and arena. Either his uncle had lied about the condition of the ranch, or the man he'd hired had been cashing the checks without doing the work.

His father's voice jumped through his head, calling him useless and lazy. Dropping to his haunches, he planted his elbows above his knees and lowered his head. The memories he tried ignoring bombarded his brain. All those years spent trying to prove himself to a father who didn't care, trying to gain approval from a man who had written him off when he was ten. A man who was now dead. Any chance of mending that relationship was gone.

In the past when these thoughts started crowding in, he'd have leaped on a bull or driven until he found a crowd that would help him drown the feelings he didn't want to deal with.

But that was getting old. A few months ago, he'd tried something new. He'd sought out Pastor Wayne, the cowboy preacher who followed the rodeo circuit. So now he prayed. He prayed for wisdom and patience.

"I'm hungry." One of his new responsibilities interrupted the prayer.

"Me, too, and I'm cold. Can we go inside?"

Even though Tomas and Isaac were a year apart at six and five, he wasn't sure who was who. What he did know was that his half brothers had started grumbling about an hour ago. All three of them. He shot a glance at the teen. Ethan had asked to come along on the road trip. Ethan's mother, the second wife, had headed back to Chicago and didn't seem to care that her son wanted to spend the holidays with three brothers he had just met at his father's funeral. Right now, the only thing that made them family was a last name. On impulse Max had thought this trip would give them a chance to connect before the little ones went to live with their aunt and Ethan returned to school.

"Max!" they cried out at the same time.

With a heavy sigh, he made sure to smile at them. It wasn't their fault, and it wouldn't be right to get mad at them. He'd seen the boys once, when they were too small to remember him. Now they had lost both parents and were stuck with brothers they didn't know, other than what they had been told.

He rubbed one of them on the head. "There are some protein bars in the truck."

"We ate them."

He glanced over his shoulder. "The whole box?"

His littlest brothers nodded in unison. That couldn't be good for their stomachs.

"Um…then get the chips. There's beef jerky, too."

"Ethan ate all those." They stood, arms crossed, mirror images of each other. The sixteen-year-old was leaning against the barn, still staring at his phone. The kid hadn't looked up once all day. Actually, Max couldn't remember seeing his eyes. Even during the funeral, he'd had his gaze glued to the small screen in his hand.

Max pinched the bridge of his nose. So far, nothing had gone right on this trip. The temperature had to have dropped twenty degrees since they left Dallas this morning.

Standing, he arched his back until he heard the popping. He winced at the pain in his shoulder. Who was he kidding? Nothing had been right for the last two months since he was stomped on by Texas Fire. He'd wanted to be the cowboy who finally stayed on that bull for a full eight seconds. He'd done it, too, but at the cost of a healthy body. One broken collarbone and one fractured eye socket were added to his already long list of wrecked body parts.

"My phone's about to die." Ethan looked up for the first time. "I need to charge it. It's like we dropped off the earth."

Max wasn't sure why the teen had even asked to join them, or why he'd agreed to it. He sighed. The kid's mother was back in Chicago. Unfortunately, Max had plenty of memories of her. She had been his first stepmother, not that she had been any kind of mother. She had sent him away to live with his mother's father. Apparently, she had no problem sending her own son away, either.

They might all have the same father, but in no way had they been part of the same household.

He hoped to not only be a better big brother but to give them a sense of family. He wanted to be a brother they could count on, even when they didn't live in the same house.

Injecting positive energy into his voice, Max smiled. "We have a couple of weeks to spend together and get some brotherly bonding. But if you want to go home, Ethan, I'm sure we can find a way to get you to the airport."

"Nah. I'm good."

Max stuffed his hands in his pockets and looked down at the two little ones. He could do this until their aunt was able to get them. He had only met Vanessa once, at the rehearsal party for his father's third marriage. She had been yelling at her sister, his father's latest bride-to-be. Wanting to stop the fiasco, she had refused to go to the wedding. Yeah, that had been a lovely moment.

She would be taking the boys as soon as she wrapped up her end-of-year work schedule. The will had listed them both as guardians. The boys were stuck with two people who were strangers to them.

He looked at Ethan again. In the new semester, the coltish kid would return to his boarding school.

In less than a month he'd be on his own again, healed up and ready to ride in the finals. He could do this. "What about the cooler? Anything left in there?"

They shook their heads again. The matching pairs of big brown eyes just about did him in. He wanted to get these pens fixed, but he didn't have the supplies he needed anyway.

"Come on, boys. We'll turn the stock out in the larger pasture, then explore the living quarters. The main brick house was built by my...our grandfather in the '70s, you know." After unloading the bulls from the trailer, they climbed back into his truck. "Our great-great-grandfather built the old ranch house over a hundred years ago. We've owned the land for almost two hundred years. When Texas was still part of Mexico."

Ethan didn't look impressed. Time and years didn't have much meaning to Isaac and Tomas. But for him? He hadn't expected this stirring of coming home.

The old path to the main house was hard to find. There wasn't any evidence that the place had had a care-taker. The weeds on the road looked as if they had grown unchecked for well over a year.

He pulled up to the house and started unloading.

"Max! Look! Someone's coming," one of the boys hollered.

Sure enough, a cloud of dust was heading their way.

Maybe if they pretended they weren't here, whoever it was would leave. There wasn't a single person in Clear Water Max wanted to see.

"Who do you think it is? Uncle Rigo said this is where our family comes from."

The other boy nodded. "He said there were lots of stupid people, too."

Great. No telling what his uncle had said to them. "That's not a nice word, guys. And Uncle Rigo is a bit grumpy, so I wouldn't listen too much to what he says."

Ethan leaned against one of the house's columns. He slipped his phone into his loose jeans, his dark hair falling over his face. "Maybe they brought food."

Max checked his watch. It was after two o'clock. Less than one day and he was already starving them. "Once this person leaves, we'll drive to Uvalde and find something to eat and get supplies."

A silver Tahoe pulled up to the front porch.

He glanced inside the vehicle. That couldn't be right. His pulse did an uptick. The one person he wanted to avoid the most had just arrived at his door. What was she doing here? He narrowed his eyes. Maybe it was her twin, Danica, and not Jackie Bergmann.

Why was she just sitting there? He tilted his head. It looked like she was talking to someone. With a nod, she got out and stood next to the SUV, a huge smile on her face…a very forced smile.

One thing was certain. It was Jackie.

The summer they had met on the rodeo circuit she had been a pretty girl, and now she was a gorgeous woman. He had hoped his teenage memories had inflated her beauty, but they hadn't. He had been Romeo to her Juliet. His stupid self had written endless poems and songs for her. Yeah, he'd been a major loser.

From that summer on, Jackie had become the standard to which he'd compared all the other women in his life. Her laugh, her quick wit, her gentleness—even her faith. To his irritation, the others had always come up short. He hated how much he had loved her. Not fun when it hadn't been returned. He seemed destined to chase after people who didn't want him.

"Hi, Max. What a good-looking family you have there. Welcome back to Clear Water." She didn't move, just stared at the two little ones standing next to him. "My. Those boys look just like you."

The one closest to him took his hand. He was the friendlier one, the one who did most of the talking. "Everyone says we're mini-Maxes. When we get our black cowboy hats, we'll be just like him. He's going to teach us how to ride bulls. He says—"

Max put a hand on the small shoulder. If he didn't cut him off now, he'd never stop talking. "Hey, Danica."

Okay, calling her by her sister's name was low, but he couldn't let her know how much she disturbed him. "What brings you out to the ranch?" He really hoped his voice sounded casual, as though seeing her again didn't uproot his foundation.

Her eyes went a little wide, then her smile relaxed. "I'm Jackie. You used to be able to tell us apart. Of course, that was a long time ago. Now it looks like you got your own twins. Congratulations on the family."

"They're not twins," he started to explain.

"He can't tell us apart, either." One of the boys giggled.

The other just watched the exchange. That had to be Tomas. He seemed to be six going on sixty.

"These are my brothers. Isaac and Tomas. That's Ethan."

"I'm five. Tomas is six. Ethan is sixteen." Isaac offered up the information with a giant smile.

"Your brothers?" Her big green eyes blinked a few times.

"Yeah, it's what happens when your father marries someone the same age as you."

"Oh. Um, I'm sorry." She looked behind her. "In town, I heard you were here with your wife and kids."

"We've been here a couple of hours, and the town gave me a family? How did they even know we were here?"

"Welcome to Smalltown, USA. And having a Delgado back on the ranch is big news."

"Well, you can let them know there's no wife. Just a band of brothers." Had she driven all the way into enemy territory to see if he was married? "How about you?"

"No brothers." The grin showed off the dimple on her right cheek. Just as quickly the smile faded, and she looked down.

That infectious grin took him back to when he was seventeen, to the time when his one goal was to get her to smile just like that. He had lived to make her laugh.

They weren't teens anymore. What was she doing out here? She had made it clear the last time they had talked that a Delgado and a Bergmann could never be together. "Are you the town's welcoming committee, or did they send you to warn us to leave, before the good townsfolk arrive with pitchforks and torches?"

Both boys looked up at him. Tomas had a deeper scowl than usual. "They don't like us?"

Max closed his eyes, wishing he had kept his mouth shut.

Jackie walked around her car and stopped at the bottom step of the house. "No. You're welcome here. Your *brother* was just trying to be funny. It's been a long time, and the ranch has been…" She twisted her mouth as her gaze swept the fences that needed repair, the overgrown pastures and the weed-covered yard.

"Neglected?" He didn't know why he was embarrassed by the condition of the ranch. Moving behind his brothers, he rubbed their heads. "We were just about to go in and inspect our living quarters. It's a bit cold out here."

"I hear you're at the top of the ranks as a Professional Bull Rider. You hit the PBR as soon as you turned eighteen."

Had she been following him? He liked the thought of that. She'd been in his thoughts just about every day since she walked away from him. No reason for her to know that.

He turned to the heavy oak door. The old key had to be jiggled a bit to fit in the knob. An odd sensation of coming home settled deep in his bones.

He shook it off. This was not home. The only reason he was here was to get the place ready to put on the market. And to get his body back into shape for the PBR finals.

Jackie's boots hit the porch. "They said the cold front would be arriving tomorrow." He could feel her right behind him. Her voice did the same strange thing to him as it used to. She continued on like it was not a big deal that they were standing so close after all these years. "Looks like they got it wrong."

It had taken years to bury thoughts of her. Now he couldn't think of anything else. "Yeah, they do that sometimes."

"The reason I came out was to talk to you about the original town plot on the edge of the ranch. It borders our ranch. The church and school are well over one hundred years old. There might be some other buildings even older. Our mothers had been working to restore them and give them back to the town as a historical site. After they…after the accident it was forgotten. I've been trying to revitalize their dream. Your father hasn't returned any of my emails, phone calls or letters. So, when I heard you were out here, I wanted to make sure I got to talk to you."

He waited, but it seemed she had finally stopped talking. Was she nervous?

"My father was down in the Caribbean for the last month. There was a boating accident. He was killed along with his wife." He nodded to the identical-looking brothers, who were now playing on the old porch swing. "Their mother."

Her mouth fell open. "Oh, Max. I'm so sorry."

"It's actually been a little over a month. No one even knew they were missing at first. Anyway, that's why he didn't get back to you."

"You have custody of the boys now?"

"Shared custody. An aunt on their mother's side will be taking them. She has a job to finish overseas, then she'll come pick them up for Christmas. Ethan is hanging with us for the holidays, then he heads back home to Chicago." He made the mistake of looking at her.

Sadness clouded her eyes as the afternoon sun glistened off the moisture that hovered on her lashes. When they had met as teens, they discovered they were both motherless, something they had in common.

But the true shock came when her father found them at the dance together. Angry, he told them that Max's mother had killed hers. The two women had been killed in the same accident here on the ranch.

After dropping that piece of news, he took Jackie away. But Max didn't want to think about their parents now, or the summer he thought he had fallen in love.

Max shoved the door open and stepped into his grandfather's home. Neglect had a smell. It was old and musty.

"This is where we're staying?" Ethan didn't look enthusiastic about the old ranch house.

Max started pulling back heavy drapes. He opened the windows. "It just needs to be aired out." He sneezed as particles filled his nose.

"Look at this!" One of the boys, Isaac maybe, tried to climb onto an old Spanish saddle that sat behind the leather sofa.

"This is so cool!" A stuffed quail was inside a glass lamp, and cowhides and antlers decorated the room. The more energetic one—the one Max thought was Isaac—ran around the large living room touching the dust-covered furniture and fixtures. The river-rock fireplace opening was taller than the boys. The dining room could be seen on the other side.

"The outlets don't work." Ethan was back to staring at his phone. He frowned. "This place is ancient. Is there even electricity?"

"Of course, there's electricity. This house was built in the early '70s. We just need to dust everything off." He flipped a switch, but the massive antler chandelier didn't light up. He walked to the other wall and flipped everything on the panel. Nothing.

Jackie had her phone out. "I'll call Mabel Horten at the co-op. She'll know if it's been turned off."

His little brothers were opening cabinets and drawers and exploring with delight. At least they hadn't complained about being hungry in front of Jackie. He needed to get food.

"Boys, be careful." They ran to the door that went to the back part of the house. "Stay where I can see you. No telling what could be living here after years of being empty."

"Cool!"

"Hi, Mabel…I need a favor. I'm out at the Delgado place…Yes, Max is in town…No, no wife. They're his brothers…Yes." She chuckled at something the person on the other end said. "Yeah, I know." Then she shook her head. "No. We're in the main house, and the lights aren't working."

He hated the thought that strangers were talking about him and the boys.

"Okay. Thanks…Yes, I'll be at the church Wednesday night. Bye." She turned to him. "It hasn't been disconnected, so maybe it's the breaker."

"I think it's in the washroom." Bits and pieces of the house returned to his memories. Cutting across the dining room and through the vast country kitchen, Jackie followed him. He glanced back to make sure the boys were okay.

"Wow, I love this kitchen." Jackie ran her hand over the old counter. "Just a few updates, and this would be a stellar place for a family."

"We're not staying that long."

The boys had gotten quiet, so he checked the living room. Ethan had pulled out a box of old record albums and flopped in a leather armchair. Isaac and Tomas crowded around him.

Going back to the kitchen, Max found Jackie standing at an open door. He followed her into the large butler's pantry. The door that led to the washroom was at the far end.

Behind the washroom door, he found the metal panel. Inside, taped tags curled, and some of them had fallen off. He flipped the longest row of switches. A loud pop came from below, and sparks flew. He threw his arm up to cover his face, and a sharp pain from his injured collarbone ran through his whole body.

Jackie gasped. "It's on fire."

Small flames danced along the wires that ran into the ceiling. Jackie ripped off her jacket and started swatting at the fire, trying to smother it. He took off his denim jacket, but she had it out before he could get his bum arm free.

She stepped back and scanned the ceiling. "That's not okay."

With the flames out, he checked the panel and made sure it was all turned off. What was he going to do now? It was getting colder, and with no heat or lights, they couldn't stay here. He pinched the bridge of his nose.

"I'll call Sammi," Jackie offered.

"Your little sister?"

"Not so little anymore. She's a genius when it comes to fixing things like this."

"Max! We're starving!" Great. Bored with the old LPs, the boys were back to being hungry.

Ethan stood behind them. "I think it's colder in here than outside."

Jackie looked at the boys. "Want to go into town to get some food? And maybe some of the best hot chocolate in the world?" She looked up at Max. "The Hill Top Café has great burgers. That'll give Sammi some time to see if she can get this working."

The boys nodded. "Yes! Please, Max?"

Ethan joined them. "I'm starving, and my phone is dead. I'm sure the restaurant has electricity."

Wow. Ethan had strung two whole sentences together. Max pushed back his hair. "I don't know. I had planned to drive to Uvalde for supplies. I thought we could get something there."

Jackie narrowed her eyes. "That's an hour away. What's wrong with buying your supplies in town? The local businesses would appreciate your shopping in Clear Water." She crossed her arms. "My family owns the local hardware store and lumberyard. There are also ranch supplies at the feed store."

With his brothers and Jackie watching him, there wasn't one single excuse he could come up with to avoid town. She was the main reason he had planned to hide out on the ranch anyway.

First the barns weren't sound, then Jackie showed up, now the house had no electricity. Even if it did, it wasn't habitable. And he was out of food. He was pretty sure Parenting 101 said something about feeding kids on a regular basis.

"Okay. Let me unhitch the trailer and we can follow in my truck."

In unison, a groan rose up from his brothers, and the matching glares from all three sets of brown eyes looked at him with the same disapproval he remembered from his father.

Jackie moved to stand next to the boys. "I came out to discuss a project we have planned for the original town buildings. Why don't you let me drive? We can talk, then order supplies. I'll text Sammi to look at the wiring. If she can't do the work, she knows who can."

"Yes. Yes! Please, Max. We're starving. We can't last another minute!" one of the boys pleaded with Max.

The other one joined in. "I'm so cold I'm turning into a icicle." Were his brothers always this dramatic? Maybe this was normal for them. He didn't even know what was normal for five- and six-year-olds. Especially when they'd lost both parents. He remembered feeling so lost and alone when his mother died, and all he had wanted was his dad. That hadn't happened. But he could be here for his brothers.

"Okay. Okay. We'll go into town with Jackie and get you fed. We've got a lot of work to do. Let's at least wash up." He went to the kitchen sink and turned the faucet. Did they even have water? The pipes sputtered and groaned, then an explosion of water came through and splashed him. Brown water.

Joining him, Ethan made a face. "Man, that's gross."

Jackie grimaced. "You might want to have the well and tank checked before you use that water. You can wash your hands at the restaurant. Sound like a plan?" She looked at him, waiting.

He gave in. "Yeah."

With a nod she turned, and his brothers fell into line, two with huge grins, and one with a bored expression. Max didn't like what he was feeling. He was surprised by the strong emotions seeing her had stirred up. He felt like a teenager again. Not cool.

All he had wanted was to get some practice in, get to know his brothers, and avoid Clear Water and anyone with the Bergmann name. Less than a day— less than three hours—and he was getting in to Jackie's car and heading in to town to have lunch with her.

The one person who probably had the power to expose his weaknesses was now sitting next to him. Coming to Clear Water had been a mistake. He would just say no to whatever she wanted and send her on her way.

Chapter Two

Jackie's hair flew across her face as she got out of the car. All the way in to town she had tried to focus on the reason she drove to the Delgado Ranch in the first place, but sitting next to Max, the guilt of the past crowded out all other thoughts.

Seeing him was more confusing than she could have imagined. It had been so many years ago. She was surprised how disappointed she had been when he had called her Danica.

People confused her and her twin all the time, but coming from Max, it had hurt. Even on the first day they had met as teenagers, he had been able to tell them apart. That had been the best summer of her life. Either they were riding or he was writing poems for her. She had been so in love and couldn't have imagined anything but a bright future for them. Until her father had found them together and she had learned who Max was. More to the point, she had discovered who his mother was.

She didn't deserve for him to remember her. Her father had unfairly blamed his mother for the accident. His hurt expression was still so clear in her mind. He hadn't said a word as her father reamed him out along with his whole family.

Not only had they both lost their mothers, they had lost them in the same car crash. She closed her eyes to block the memory, but the look of betrayal on Max's face still took up too much space. He had just stood there. Alone.

Her father had made sure that had been the last time she saw him. That was a long time ago. They had been kids, and he obviously had gotten over her. If she wanted to have access to the original settlement, she would have to bury the past.

The buildings. From the records and her mother's letters, there was an old church, school and general mercantile, along with several other buildings. She needed his permission to move them off the ranch to the land the city had granted for the project. What would be the best angle to get Max on board with her plan?

One step ahead of her, he went to open the door. A short gust of wind pushed it out of Max's hand as they hurried inside. "The weather's getting worse." His voice was muffled in the zipped-up Carhartt jacket.

"Too cold to stay out at your place without heat." The air burned her throat with each breath. "You might need to make plans to stay somewhere else tonight. The Pecan Farm has cabins. I could call Maggie for you."

"A cabin?" Ethan sounded suspicious.

"We've always wanted to go camping. Are there bears by the cabin?" Isaac hopped around. "That would be so cool. Right, Tomas?"

Jackie laughed as she moved past him. "No. No bears, but there are deer, raccoons and a river where you could fish. If this weather keeps up, we might have ice fishing for the first time in Texas." She pointed out the bathrooms before leading them to her favorite booth in front of the large window.

A young waitress with a huge smile brought a basket of tortilla chips and a bowl of salsa. The boys attacked the food like they hadn't eaten in a week.

"How are you, Kelsey?" Jackie was looking at the girl, but Kelsey was glancing at Ethan from under her lashes.

"Hi, Ms. Bergmann. Is it cold enough for you?" She never took her gaze off the teen. He didn't seem to notice. He was frowning at his dead phone.

Rubbing her hands together before tucking them in her jacket, Jackie smiled up at her. "I don't remember it ever being this cold in November."

"Yeah, it's a record breaker. What a cute crew you have with you today. What can I get for you to drink? Coffee and hot chocolate?"

Jackie leaned closer to the young brothers. "I recommend the hot chocolate. That's what I'm getting."

The little ones looked at Max. He nodded. "Three hot chocolates and one coffee."

Ethan looked up from plugging in his charger, and when his eyes widened, Max raised a brow.

The teen's expression took Jackie right back to the summer with Max. Ethan looked so much like him. The Delgados definitely had a look.

He pushed his hair back and grinned at the waitress. "Hi, I'm Ethan. I'd give anything for a Mocha Frappuccino with organic, unsweetened almond milk."

"Hi. I would love to have one, too, but all my mom serves is plain coffee. Plain cream and sugar are the only options. I could put some Cool Whip from the desserts on top."

"We want whipped cream on our hot chocolates!" Isaac pointed to his brother. Tomas nodded in agreement.

"Sure." She looked back at Ethan. "I make the hot chocolate myself with real ingredients. It's my favorite."

Max's brother blushed. "I'll take one of those."

"Good. So, are y'all visiting or moving to town?" It seemed as if everyone else at the table had disappeared as the two teens stared at each other. "Are you gonna go to school here? Everyone's out for Thanksgiving break, but Monday we start again."

Jackie cleared her throat. "Kelsey, this is Max Delgado and his brothers—Tomas, Isaac and of course Ethan. They're in town for a short break, and right now they're hungry. Could you give us the menus?"

A red flush covered Kelsey's face as she tucked her chin. "Sorry. I'll get the drinks." She laid laminated menus on the table and hurried away.

A short time later, the owner of the café sat chips and salsa on the table. She didn't look happy, but then again Sally Pryce was famous for good food. Friendliness? Not so much.

"Hi, Sally. Max, this is Sally Pryce, the owner and Kelsey's mother and my cousin. Sally, this is—"

"Yes, I heard a Delgado was back in town. I'll be serving your table while you're here." She narrowed her eyes at Ethan. "Kelsey is my only daughter, and she has five older brothers. And since you're just going to be here a short time, I recommend you take care of the ranch. I hear the thistle is out of control. I'll have your drinks out soon."

As soon as she had her back to them, Ethan narrowed his eyes at Max. "What was that about? Did Dad or Uncle Rigo do something to make the people here hate us?"

Max looked at Jackie. "It's complicated, and it's the reason I wanted to go to Uvalde. No one hates us there." Max leaned in and looked straight at Ethan. "Our father and uncle made some decisions that weren't popular here, along with a few other issues." He looked at Jackie, but quickly glanced away.

Jackie folded her hands in front of her. "It's not just your father and uncle. It goes way back before anyone here was even alive. There's been bad blood between the Delgado family and Clear Water for as long as anyone can remember. It has to do with the old land charter for the town. Most recently, everyone blames y'all for the thistle outbreak."

"Thistle outbreak? Is that some sort of disease?" Ethan stared at her.

"No, it's a plant that is prickly and large. It has a thousand little seeds that will take over a pasture and kill off the grass." She looked at Max. "Rumor is that your mother had over a hundred bird feeders around the house and barns. The birdseed she ordered from Kerrville had it in the mix. With the land not being tended, it's become a battle on the other ranches."

Max's mouth fell open. "You're serious? They blame my mother? She's been gone for twenty years."

Jackie didn't know how to answer that. The guilt she already felt over his mother's death didn't help. "Small towns have long memories."

"That's not fair." Ethan leaned back and looked out the window. "Not that it's a big surprise they hate us. We don't even like each other."

"We like you." Isaac smiled at his brother. Tomas nodded, but his heartbreakingly sad expression tore at her heart.

Ethan glared at the younger boys. "You don't even know me."

"You're our brother." They both looked confused. To them it was simple. They were family.

"You're too young to understand anything. This is so lame." The teenager threw himself against the cushioned back of the booth and crossed his arms.

Max pinched the bridge of his nose.

Jackie wanted to reach out and hug all the boys close to her. To tell them that God loved them and that was all that mattered, but she didn't even know where they were in their faith. Maybe she could help by refocusing them. "You're right, Ethan. It's not fair. This is one of the reasons I came out to the ranch. I have a plan that might help restore goodwill for the Delgados here in town."

Ethan and Max made an identical grunting noise at the exact same time.

Biting her tongue to stop the laugh, she had to smile at their matching sullen expressions. She leaned closer to Max. "The original town church and school are on your property. I would love to move them into town and restore the buildings. The city has land set aside. I don't need anything from you other than permission. It's what our mothers were working on when—"

"Sorry." Max cut her off. "My uncle asked me to get the ranch ready for sale, and I have orders to clear out the pastures and tear down any old buildings. He wants the old wood sent to him."

Adrenaline rushed through her heart. Her brain rebelled at the horror of tearing down the buildings. But before she could protest, Dub Childress walked over to their table.

His glare fixed on Max. "You're the oldest Delgado

grandson. Maximiliano, right?" He pronounced it with the Spanish accent.

Max stood and held out his hand. "Yes, sir. These are my brothers. Ethan, Isaac and Tomas."

He nodded, shaking Max's hand. "Are your father or uncle coming into town?"

"No, sir. My uncle has obligations that keep him in Dallas. My father passed away last month. Boating accident."

Dub's face tightened. "Sorry to hear that. Are you making plans to clear out the thistles?"

"I'll see what I can do."

Sally came to the table with a tray full of hot drinks. Dub nodded and moved back to his seat. "Now, what can I get y'all to eat?"

Max looked at his brothers. "Are burgers and fries good for everyone?"

They all nodded.

With the joy gone out of their faces, Isaac and Tomas took the mugs and just stared at the fluffy white topping. It wasn't their fault. Jackie wanted to help them but wasn't sure what to do.

She tucked her hands under her thighs. "I'm sorry."

Max stared into his black coffee. "Not your problem. It goes with the territory of being a Delgado."

Silence fell over the table after Sally left with their orders. Ethan had gone back to staring at his newly charged phone. Max laid his arm on the back of the bench as he sipped his coffee.

She had to try again. "Surely your uncle doesn't actually want to destroy the buildings."

"No. He's opening a new store north of Dallas in Flower Mound. It's not just the 'biggest'—" he made air quotes "—Western store in the country. The newest Delgado Cowboy Central will be an experience. He wants to re-create an authentic Western town inside the store. I wouldn't even call it a store. It's more like a football stadium, a destination."

"But those buildings belong here in Clear Water."

Tomas and Isaac started jostling each other. If they'd driven in from Dallas today, they must have been sitting a long time. Her nieces would have been going crazy by now.

"Do you guys like old-fashioned arcade games?"

The corner of Max's mouth lifted. "I've been known to do a pretty mean pinball. Hey, guys. You want to go old-school and play in the arcade?" He reached for his wallet and took out some cash.

"Like stuff from the '80s?" Ethan looked up.

"Probably." Max and Jackie answered at the same time.

With a lopsided grin, Max nodded to Ethan. "Will you take your brothers while we wait for the food?"

Before Max could move out of the booth, the boys crawled under the table and ran to the back room. Ethan followed with much less energy.

"Walk," Max yelled after them, but they didn't seem to hear. "I have no idea what I'm doing. I thought it was time we got to know each other, spend some time together. I'm starting to think this was a very bad idea. I get so angry at my father. He created this mess, and now I can't even yell at him. I don't know anything about kids, especially grieving ones."

"No, your brothers need you. They're young. They don't understand what's going on. Ethan, well, he's a teenager. They're not good at expressing what they need because they're confused in general. You're doing the right thing." Without thinking about it, she reached across the table and covered his hand with hers. "You've all had a loss, and they need family right now. So do you."

He snorted. "My father didn't build a loving community with his kids. It was more or less every man for himself. People are easily discarded in the Delgado clan."

"You can make your own choices." She remembered the sensitive boy she had fallen in love with. "I know you're not your father, Max. Do you still write?"

"No. You don't know me anymore. We were kids back then. We didn't know anything, let alone who we were."

She pulled back. "If you don't like the way your father was, then change. God created you in His image. You don't have to carry on your father's legacy. With God, you can start new, you and your brothers." She looked down. He didn't want to be preached at. "Sorry."

"Don't be." His gaze stayed focused on the slow-moving town outside the window. "Pastor Wayne said pretty much the same thing." A cold wall fell between them that had nothing to do with the weather outside.

The hard jaw flexed as his attention touched her briefly before moving away again. "Listen, I know what you want, and I can't deliver. My uncle is in charge now, and he wants the wood salvaged and sent to Flower Mound. More people will see them there if that makes you happy." He shrugged. "That's where they're going, and there's nothing I can do about it."

She pulled back. What had she been thinking? Maybe everything her father said about the Delgado family was true and Max wasn't the sweet boy of her memories. It was all about what they could sell or who they could use. They didn't care about their history.

Leaning forward, she crossed her arms and looked him straight in the eye. He was going to learn what it meant to be a Bergmann. "I'm not giving up that easily. Get me in touch with your uncle. I'm sure we can work out some sort of deal. Maybe some positive PR." Her heart pounded in her ears. This was her gift to her mother. To finish the work her mother had started. So many years working on this project. It couldn't come down to one simple no.

"Max, the history is so important to protect and preserve. It won't cost y'all any money. I have grants and city support. I've been working on this a long time. I just need the buildings. They belong to Clear Water. It's what my mother—" she bit her lip "—and your mother wanted."

"Don't go there. What does it matter anyway? Saving the buildings won't bring them back."

Leaning closer, she looked him right in the eyes. A couple of inches separated them. "History is how we remember where we came from."

He rested his arm on the back of the booth, trying to act as if he didn't have a care in the world, but she could see the pulse at the base of his neck, in the space near his collarbone. "There's your problem. With my family's past? I would rather forget. My parents are gone, and I'd rather plunge in to the future. History belongs behind us."

She wasn't sure what to say to that. "How can you not want to honor them?" Her voice sounded rough to her own ears. "I'll never forget my mother. This was important to her. And to yours." He had to understand. "The boy I spent that summer with would have understood."

"That boy is long gone." He pinned her with a stare. His once-warm eyes now stared coldly at her, as though they were strangers. "Jackie, some rotted-out buildings are not going to bring them back. Is that what this is all about? Our mothers?"

Yes. No. She couldn't think. Before she could respond, Sally was passing out plates full of giant burgers and hand-cut fries. "Anything else I can get y'all?"

Jackie smiled and thanked her, her face stinging from embarrassment and unshed tears. She had lost her appetite. There was no way she could eat a bite. "Yes, I'd like a to-go box."

Max stood. "I'll get the boys. If we could get it all to go, that'd be great." He glanced at Jackie, then looked off to where the boys had gone. "You can take us back to the ranch. I'll go to Uvalde for our supplies."

Sally shot a frown his way, and a few of the people around the café cut hostile stares at him as he walked to the back to get the boys.

She wasn't going to feel sorry for him.

Once and for all, Max Delgado was out of her heart and gone from her thoughts. He had been hiding in the deepest part of her subconscious without her even being aware he was there. It was good that he was here and she could let go of any teenage fantasy.

She could focus on what was important. Getting those buildings restored. Their mothers had wanted this for the town and their families. She wanted this for them, so they would never be forgotten. Maybe some of the guilt would finally fade away.

She finished her hot chocolate and pushed back her cup.

Ignoring the suspicious glares, Max stood in the archway and scanned the small game room located between the café and the convenience store on the other side of the building. He hated the feelings Jackie brought out in him. He didn't want to think about his mother or his father. Especially his father. It wouldn't change anything. He'd just get angry, and he was tired of living with anger.

Ethan was in a race car simulator. Max didn't see Tomas or Isaac. "Where are the boys?"

The lanky teen leaned to the right, then pulled to the left. "They said they had to go to the bathroom."

"You let them go by themselves?" He was not in the mood for this. Pulling in a deep breath, he forced his voice to remain calm. No need to take his frustration out on Ethan.

"They seemed old enough to be potty trained." Ethan yelled at the screen and jerked left.

Max wasn't in the mood for the teen's sarcasm. He spotted the large restroom sign next to the soda counter. "This is a public gas station. You don't let them go off on their own. I put you in charge of them."

Ethan slammed his palms against the faux steering wheel as his race car came in last. With a grumble, he finally looked at Max. "Maybe I don't want to be in charge. That's your job. You volunteered for babysitting duty. I didn't."

Max gritted his teeth. He wanted to point out that Ethan had asked to come along; no one had invited him. But even though his knowledge was limited when it came to kids, he knew that getting into a power struggle with a teenager was an exercise in futility.

Stepping into the public restroom, he knocked on the stall doors. "Tomas! Isaac!"

No answer came back to him. Glancing under the doors, he found the stalls empty. Sheer panic froze him in place for a moment. They had to be here. Horror stories of kids disappearing swamped his brain. That kind of stuff didn't happen in Clear Water, not here in Smalltown, USA. "Tomas! Isaac!"

They had to be here somewhere. Coming out of the bathroom, he walked briskly over to the convenience store side. The boys would love to play with the souvenirs and toys over there. Maybe they'd wandered that way. "Ethan! They aren't in here. Get Jackie. I'm going to see if they went into the store."

Ethan stood, his mouth open. "What do you mean? They have to be there."

Max took a deep breath to keep himself from yelling. "They're gone. Tell Jackie." Without waiting, he rushed over to find a clerk who might have seen the boys.

His mind was racing with all the worst possibilities. The kid organizing chip bags looked all of sixteen. "Did you see two boys? Dark hair. Identical looking. Five and six years old? They were in the restroom."

"No, but I heard the bell over the door a little bit ago." He frowned. "Do you need me to call the sheriff?"

"Maybe." Was he overreacting? No, they were small kids, and they were missing. "Yeah. I'll go outside and check."

"Max?" Jackie charged into the store from the café. Ethan was close behind. "What do you need me to do?"

"He's calling the sheriff. I'm going outside."

"Okay. We'll find them." Her matter-of-fact tone helped him calm down.

"Y'all need help?" Some of the people from the café joined them.

Jackie turned to the small group. "The boys didn't come back from the restroom."

Max didn't wait around to hear the rest of the conversation. Out the front door, he turned to the right. It looked like a drive-through feed store. Bags of feed were stacked on pallets, and bales of hay lined the opposite side.

Behind the hay, he heard familiar giggling. His knees went weak at the beautiful sound.

"There they are." Ethan's voice didn't sound steady.

They were safe. For a moment, all Max wanted to do was sink to the floor and cover his face. That had to have been the worst experience of his life. More terrifying than any bull he'd ever faced.

He moved round the bales. The brothers sat in the middle of a pen, smiling, surrounded by a litter of puppies.

He took what felt like his first breath since going into the restroom. Someone touched his arm. Turning, he found Jackie next to him. She wasn't wearing a jacket, but her smile was warm. The people who had been in the café crowded into the feed store area.

Her hand slipped down to his. "They're okay."

He managed a nod. She left him and joined the group of people at the entrance. "He found them with the puppies. Thanks for offering to help."

Dub nodded. "Happy that they're safe. I'll call dispatch and let them know we don't need the sheriff." The small crowd went back to the warm café.

"Great. Now they think I'm the worst guardian, along with all the other things they condemn the Delgados for."

"Kids slip away. It happens to a lot of good parents. It is terrifying, but they're safe. That's all that matters."

"I'm not their parent."

"For now, you're the only parent they have."

That stopped him cold. He hadn't thought of it that way. They were his responsibility. He wanted to give them more than his father had given him, but he wasn't sure he knew how. Rubbing the back of his neck, he turned back to the boys. Ethan had a tight grip on the top of the temporary pen.

He didn't trust himself to join them yet. Ethan needed to be aware of the consequences of being careless, and Isaac and Tomas had to understand they couldn't wander off. But if he started talking to them now, he feared he'd start yelling and criticizing. That's what his father would have done, so he'd start by not doing that. He needed to calm down before they had that conversation.

He took a deep breath, and a gust of cold air seared his lungs.

Who was he kidding? All that stuff about being their parent and being better than his father was a joke. There was no way he could do this. He just wanted to get out of Clear Water. Let his uncle deal with the ranch. Jackie and her buildings were not his problems. They couldn't be.

Chapter Three

Once her heart returned to a reasonable beat, Jackie kneeled at the edge of the enclosure that held the litter of rambunctious puppies. Next to her, Ethan gripped the top of the wire panel that made a temporary pen. His shoulders rose and fell with each hard breath. It looked like he was breathing fire when his exhalation hit the cold air. The color had left the teen's face.

"You told me you were going to the restroom!" he started yelling at the twins. "You can't just leave like that." His voice cracked. "What were you thinking?" His pitch went higher.

"Ethan." Max walked up next to him and placed a hand on the center of his back. "We'll talk about this later."

The teen's nostrils flared as he shook his head. "Someone bad could have kidnapped you. The people in the café had to call the police!"

Tomas ducked his head. Tears built in his eyes as he hugged the puppy.

"Stop, Ethan." Max's stern voice left no room for argument. "We'll talk about this later, and we'll also address your responsibility in this. They're little kids.

You're older." He cut a glance at the boys. "We *will* talk about this." He looked back at Ethan. "In private."

The black fluff ball that Tomas held against his chest stopped wriggling and licked the boy's face. He kept his eyes down.

Isaac looked down at the golden puppy in his lap. "There's lots of cool stuff here, then we heard the puppies bark," he mumbled. The usually happy brother was also on the verge of tears. "Momma said she was bringing home a puppy for Christmas."

Jackie covered her mouth. These babies had lost both parents and had been left with brothers they didn't even know. Swinging her leg over the panel, she joined the boys in the middle of the litter.

She sat between them. Maybe she was overstepping, but she pulled them close. Two other puppies joined them, jumping over each other, tails wagging.

With a soft squeeze, she pressed a kiss to the side of each of the boys' heads. "We were worried about you. You must let your brothers know where you're at all the time. They love you, and were scared when they couldn't find you."

Isaac looked up at Ethan and Max. "We're sorry. Look." He held his pup up to them. "This one has the same color of hair as Momma, and that one is the same as Daddy. They were waiting for us."

Tomas wiped his face across his sleeve and smiled at the puppy that licked him. "They need homes. Can we take them? Maybe they're the dogs Momma was going to give us."

Max blew out a heavy sigh and ran his hands through his hair. "I'm sorry, boys, but it'll be up to Vanessa. You're going to be living with her."

Silent tears fell to the concrete, leaving prints in the

dust. Tomas buried his face in the soft fur. Jackie looked at Max. He had his hands stuffed in his back pockets. The muscles in his jaw popped. There had to be something they could do. Ethan joined them, sitting cross-legged, and a few of the puppies scrambled into his lap.

"Hey, folks. Jim McClain." The feed store owner joined them. He wiped his hands with a bandanna before offering one in greeting to Max. "If you want them, those puppies will be ready to go home with you by the end of the week. The two smaller ones are the only homeless ones. They're my sister's dogs. The mother is a super sweet Lab. Good family dog." He grinned. "Not sure about the father. I think he might be the neighbor's Australian shepherd. They're real smart. Easy to train. Already house broke. Looks like a perfect match to me."

"We're just here temporarily." Max frowned.

Jim looked down. "Jackie! Hey, girl, what are you doing? Your dad need any hay or feed? Maybe a couple of dogs?" He laughed.

Jim towered over Max and was twice his size. He had played college ball and was now back in town running the family business. He was always trying to get her to buy something or go on a date with him. She had been able to avoid both by avoiding the feed store altogether, until now.

She smiled. "No thanks, Jim. This is Tomas and Isaac Delgado and their brothers, Ethan and Max."

Eyes narrowed, Jim crossed his massive arms. "Thought you looked familiar. Your uncle had all his feed and hay shipped in from Kerrville. You here to clear out all those thistles? They're ruining all our grass."

She stood. "Jim, he's here with his brothers because their father died in an accident. He's looking to clean up the land and get it back into shape."

Max glared at her. "I don't need to explain myself or my brothers to anyone."

Isaac stood, holding his puppy close. "Mr. McClain, we'd take really good care of these two. We think they want to stay together, so they won't be scared when they leave their mom."

Jim softened and smiled at the five-year-old. "I believe they like you, too. I'll talk to my sister, and you talk with your brother. It's a big responsibility." He went down on his haunches so that he was eye to eye with both boys. "They'd count on you to take care of them."

The brothers now stood next to each other, each hugging a puppy like they'd never let go. Tomas kissed his black pup on its nose. "We're going to call this one Baby. That's what Momma called Daddy."

Isaac giggled as the golden pup licked his ear. "This one is going to be Queenie because Daddy called Momma his queen. She's blonde like Momma. What do you think?"

Jim patted the little dog. "Those sound like fine names." He stood and turned to Max. "Looks like you got a couple of dogs. I can put all the supplies you'll need on a ranch account for you." He turned to the boys. "On that second aisle over there is a bunch of collars and other stuff puppies need. Pick out what you want, and I'll have it all ready for you when you pick them up the Saturday after Thanksgiving." He smirked at Max. "I trust you'll pay the balance then."

Rushing over the fencing, the twins charged into Max. "Please. We love these puppies. Vanessa'll love them, too."

He looked at Jackie, a sadness in his eyes. She thought about pointing out to the boys that Max hadn't actually agreed to them keeping the dogs. With a sigh, he shook his head.

Ethan scowled. "You're going to let them do whatever they want, aren't you?"

Max dropped to meet the boys eye to eye. "I'm so sorry, boys, but we can't take these puppies. If Vanessa says no, then they will have nowhere to go. That's not fair to them." He reached out to wipe a tear off Isaac's cheek. "It's not fair to you, either. I can't tell you yes, then turn around and take them away from you."

Tomas squeezed his puppy. "We could all stay with you."

The sadness in Max's eyes caused her to fight back her own tears. There had to be some way she could help. Maybe she could offer to take the puppies.

Max picked up one of the puppies. "Tomas, I'll be going back to the rodeo soon. We have the next couple of weeks together, then you'll be going with Vanessa. We'll visit and talk as much as you want, but you can't live with me. Do you understand?"

"Yes, sir." Both boys nodded.

He looked at Jim. "Maybe we could visit while we're still in town?"

"Not a problem. The puppies always need a bit of attention." Jim held his hand out again and waited for Max to take it. "Welcome back to Clear Water, Delgado. Let me know what you need, and I can have it delivered. If you need help clearing out the thistles, I know where you can hire some local boys." He pulled a card out of his shirt pocket. "Call me for whatever you need."

"Thanks." Max didn't look all that thankful. "Come on, boys. Tell the dogs bye. We need to get our food and head to the ranch. I don't need you getting sick from being out in the cold." He turned to her as he pulled off his jacket. "Here, put this on. You can't get sick, either. Don't need more reasons for people to hate me."

"I come from tough stock." She pulled the comfortable denim around her shoulders anyway and tried not to inhale his scent too deeply. It filled her with comfort. Not good. "But thank you."

He watched as she gently helped the boys put the puppies back with the litter. Caring for the boys, and giving them what they needed, seemed to come naturally for her.

Why is it so hard for me? It would be easier to face down an angry bull than tell these boys no.

A few more tears and they said their goodbyes. Going back through the convenience store to the café, they gathered their food and got everyone buckled in to her car.

Not a word was spoken as they drove down Main Street. Early signs of Christmas had already appeared in some of the shop windows. The holidays were just around the corner. It had pretty much been just another day in his life.

Isaac slurped his drink. "When can we visit the puppies again?"

Jackie made eye contact through the rearview mirror, then glanced at Max.

Ethan shook his head. "Are we going to talk about what they did?" He leaned forward and glared at the boys. "You took off without telling me where you were going. You caused a lot of trouble."

Jackie stopped at the only light in town. She looked at Max as if she expected him to do something. He was tired, and he didn't know how to fix any of this.

"Ethan, when I sent you with the boys, I expected

you to watch them. They're only five and six and in a strange place. Maybe I need to take your phone, so you'll remember your responsibilities."

Horror etched itself on the teen's face. "You can't do that! You don't pay the bill. My mom does."

"If you want to return to your mom, that wouldn't be a problem. I can hire a driver to take you to the airport, and you can go back to Chicago."

Crossing his arms, Ethan stared out the window. "So, I lose my phone because they ran off. They don't even have phones, so what's going to happen to them? I told them to come right back, and they didn't listen to me."

Isaac twisted around. "No, you didn't say anything. You were playing a game."

"You didn't check on them. That was your job." He looked at the tiny versions of himself. "Guys, you can't ever disappear like that again. If you had gotten hurt or lost, we wouldn't have known where to find you."

"Like Momma and Daddy on the boat? They didn't tell anyone, and no one knew they were lost. Could we have died like them?"

Ethan leaned over his seat from the back. "Yes! That's why you can't go off by yourselves."

Tomas looked like he was about to start crying again.

"Ethan!" Saying this sharper and angrier than he had meant, Max closed his eyes for a minute and counted before addressing the teen again. "Scaring them is not the way to go."

"Well, they scared me! And now you want to take away my phone." He threw himself back. "This isn't fair. I don't want to go back to Chicago." He twisted his mouth and glared out the window.

Oh, man, it looks like he is about to cry. "You don't want to go home with your mother?"

"Do you want me to leave?"

"No. But it's going to be Thanksgiving. I thought you might want to be with your family. Don't you have stepbrothers?" He still wasn't too sure why Ethan had asked to come with them.

"Yes. I'd rather be here without my phone than being forced to hang out with them. I'd sleep in the barn if I have to. They're not nice, and my stepfather thinks… everything they do is funny."

Jackie looked up. "What about your mother?"

He shrugged and looked out the window. "She's busy."

Max closed his eyes. And scrambled some ideas around in his brain. He could figure this out. The reason he had taken the boys and why he'd let Ethan join them was that he remembered the loneliness after his mother's death. Like the world had gone on and forgotten her and him.

With her gone, he didn't exist anymore. Then he forgot her. He didn't want that for his brothers.

It sounded as if Ethan's mother wasn't any better than their father. He didn't have any warm memories of her; it didn't sound like she was any better with her own son. "Okay, here's the deal. Extra chores for everyone, and Ethan's in charge. I'll make up a list, and each day for the next week you'll make sure everything gets done before bedtime. Got it?"

Ethan looked at him. "I get to stay and keep my phone?"

"Yes, but you're going to have limited use of the phone. It's going to be hard work."

"That's okay. It's not like I have anything else to do."

He wanted to give them more than chores and work.

"I also need each of you to make a list of your favorite things to do that don't include electronics."

The younger brothers started talking over each other about swimming, food fights and playing fetch. Which they pointed out would require a dog.

Jackie pulled up to the elaborate iron gate that marked the entrance to the Delgado Ranch. When Max had first arrived with the boys, he'd found the electric rollers jammed. It had taken all four of them to push both sides back. Now the rusted curves and cattle cutouts sat lop-sided in the tall weeds. He should have turned back then and there.

He needed to call Vanessa about the dogs. In the meantime, he was going to find ways for them to have fun. Glancing at the woman driving, he thought back to that summer so long ago. He wanted to see that smile again. When had she become so severe?

Behind him, Isaac and Tomas had fallen asleep. Something else he needed to do. Make sleeping arrangements. They couldn't stay in the house tonight. If it were just him, he'd sleep in his truck. He'd done it several times. He glanced behind him at his three brothers. But for now, it wasn't just him.

How had this become his life? He leaned his head back and shut his eyes. He could do this. It was temporary.

Jackie pulled up behind Sammi's truck at the Delgado ranch house. "The boys fell asleep. I have a few blankets in the back of the car. If you want to get Tomas, I'll grab Isaac."

Max nodded before he got out of the SUV. "I think it's gotten colder." They leaned in at the same time and unbuckled the boys. She avoided looking at Max. They were too close, and parts of her heart were stirring. Not acceptable. She had forced him out of her heart years ago; she couldn't allow him back in.

She turned to Ethan. "Grab those blankets behind the seat there."

Just like the family she used to fantasize about, they made their way up the front walkway carrying the sleeping boys into the house. Of course, in her daydreams the furniture wasn't covered in dust and neglect and her heart in guilt.

For years, it had been Max she saw in those dreams. It took persistence and hard work to get him out of her head. Unfortunately, he had grown up even better looking than her imagination, but he still wasn't the right one for her.

Her feelings had to be buried the moment her father informed her who he was. He lost his mother because of her. Even if he could still like her, she didn't deserve his love.

If he ever found out the accident was her fault, he would hate her. That might be better. Now that he was back, those long-buried dreams had found their way to the surface.

Ethan opened the door. Inside, they settled the boys on the sofas and covered them with the clean afghans and quilts. She said a soft prayer for the little guys and their big brothers. Looking up, she found Max staring at her and quickly turned away.

She needed God's guidance in all of this. It felt as if she was walking on dangerous ground with hidden trip wires ready to blow everything up.

In the washroom, they found the ladder from the crawl space pulled down. "Sammi? Are you up there?"

After a few thumps and some other noises, the youngest Bergmann sister peeked over the edge of the trapdoor. "Yep. It's a mess up here. You got a whole colony of squirrels that need to be relocated, and they've been chewing on the wiring."

She disappeared.

Max sighed. "This is all I need. Squatter squirrels and a house that has to have all the wiring redone."

Sammi's boot appeared on the top of the ladder. "It's not the whole house, but I do suggest you get a licensed electrician to check it out." She hopped off the last step and turned to face them. "Hi, I'm Sammi Bergmann." She held out her hand. "Pleasure to meet you."

Ethan had come up behind Max. "Really? You know we're Delgados, right?" Bitterness laced his words.

Sammi chuckled. "That's okay. My last name might be Bergmann but everyone around here, including my family, refers to my mother as—" she lifted her hand to make air quotes "—'that other woman.' Or 'the mistake.'"

Jackie gasped. "No one blames you or loves you any less because of what your mother did to Daddy. She left you, too."

"Right. I know that. I'm just saying I don't blame people for things that happened in the past or what other people did. Unfortunately, for the most part small towns don't follow that train of thought. I think it's from the lack of real entertainment." She turned back to Max and Ethan with a smile. "How long are y'all in town?"

"Until Christmas. Or sooner. Depends on when the boys' aunt can pick them up, and how long it takes to get the ranch ready for the market."

Her eyes went wide. "You're selling this place? Hasn't it been in your family like, forever?"

"Yes. But my uncle wants the ranch gone. He and my father argued all the time. Now that my father's dead, there's nothing to stop my uncle Rigo from cleaning house and getting rid of any properties not contributing to the family coffers."

"Sorry to hear about your father. So close to the holidays, too."

"Thanks."

Jackie leaned on the edge of the old washer. "You're a Delgado. Don't you have as much say as your uncle? You know, donating the buildings would be a great Christmas gift to the town. I just don't understand why your uncle is so set against retaining Clear Water's history."

Ethan snorted. "Our uncle hated our dad." He looked at Max. "Can we go see the buildings? There have to be some creepy stories in an old abandoned town. I'm going to put that on my list of fun stuff to do. Maybe someone would want to open a dude ranch in a ghost town."

Sammi chuckled and headed into the kitchen. "That sounds entertaining, but I need to get back to the lumberyard. Sorry I wasn't more help."

They followed her into the large kitchen. She reached into her back pocket and pulled out a small pad of yellow paper. With a pencil, she wrote something out. "Here's the name and number of a guy that can help you with the wiring. I've also added Danica's number. She does animal rescue, so she'll know the best way to move the family in the attic." Handing him the paper, she tucked the pad back into her pocket. "With the house in this shape, I don't think you'll be in before the holidays. With it only being five days away, it'll be hard to find people to come out. What are your plans for Thanksgiving? It'll be a hard one. The first family holiday without your father."

Max shook his head. "I don't remember ever spending Thanksgiving with my father, but I'm worried about

Tomas and Isaac. They're little and haven't had time to be ignored by him yet." He looked at Ethan. "What do y'all normally do?"

Leaning on the counter, the teenager frowned. "I don't know what they do. I was three when my parents divorced, and I've never been invited to spend it with the Delgados."

Sammi laid her hand over her heart. "Oh, no! That's not right. My family might be a little rough around the edges, but we're always together for the holidays. You should join us. Our nieces are about the age of the boys. No one should be alone for Thanksgiving. Jackie, they should come over, shouldn't they?"

Jackie's heart picked up speed. Max couldn't come to her house. But not a single good reason came to mind and just saying no made her sound petty.

The corner of Max's mouth went up. "She's trying to think of a polite way to not invite us. Thanks, Sammi, but I'm pretty sure your father would barricade us from your home."

"Daddy can seem pretty grumpy, but we have an open-door policy." Sammi smiled at Ethan. "My father can't hold what your uncle and father did against you, and he would never deny kids a real Thanksgiving. We have all the trimmings and always twice as much food as we need."

All the problems formed a wall in Jackie's brain. And they weren't entirely about upsetting her father: Joaquin would be there. "Sammi, what about Joaquin?" Jackie couldn't believe her sister would put her best friend in such an awkward situation on Thanksgiving Day. Everyone in town knew Rigo Delgado was Joaquin's biological father, even if the man refused to acknowledge it. As far as she knew, he was still married with two daughters about the same age as Joaquin. And that man had the nerve to hold a grudge against Clear Water. No one in town would welcome him.

Sammi's eyes went wide. "Oh." She glanced at Max.

"Joaquin? Someone I know?" he asked.

Her sister's features stiffened, but she shook her head at Max and answered her sister. "He's actually a big fan of Max's. He's followed his career." She turned back to Max. "Joaquin Villarreal. Do you know who he is?"

Jackie watched his expression. He didn't react.

"Is he PBR, too?" Max had a look of total confusion on his face.

Jackie glared at her little sister. "He's a family friend who works for our dad when he's not riding the circuit. He's a PRCA cowboy," she glanced at Ethan. "That's Professional Rodeo Cowboy Association, but he hasn't made it into the top twenty."

"Yet." Now Sammi sent a hostile look back at her sister. "He's been close."

"Does he ride bulls? I need to get some practice in. Maybe we could join up." Max cleared his throat. "I feel there is something I should know. What am I missing?"

Should I tell him? She sighed. It was Joaquin's business, but it was just one more reason her father didn't like the Delgado family.

Instead of answering him, Jackie moved to the living room, where the little boys were curled up under her blankets. "Do you need any help getting a cabin at The Pecan Farm?"

He was right behind her. "If you can give me a number, I'll call. I have a few more things to do around here, then we'll head out." He stuffed his hands in his pockets. "Thanks for the invite, Sammi, but I think we'll stick to a quiet dinner."

Jackie tried to hide her relief, but from the twist of Max's mouth she might not have been as successful as she hoped. She hated being rude, but having Max there would bring up too many raw emotions for too many people.

Then again, the idea of them eating sandwiches in a lonely cabin tore at her heart.

Max moved closer, less than six inches from her. The scent of leather, denim and autumn surrounded her. He even smelled like a man without trying.

Lifting her chin, she met his stare. "You can bring the boys over if you think they would enjoy a big family Thanksgiving."

"I doubt they've ever had an experience like that."

"Ohh." Heavy sadness dripped from Sammi's one word. "You have to bring them."

He moved away from Jackie and went to the living room. Bending over the sofa, he checked the boys. "We came out here to spend time getting to know each other. A simple dinner is perfect for us. It's just another day in the scheme of things." Facing the sisters, Max rested on the back of the couch and crossed his ankles. "Thanks for the help, Sammi. I'll make sure to call those numbers."

She grabbed her coat. "Anytime. And if you need anything, don't think twice about calling me. You can find whatever you need at the lumberyard. If we don't have it, we can order it."

Jackie wanted to stay but didn't have one single reason she should.

She looked at the old fireplace. Without a fire it was cold and empty. "You might want to find some wood if you stay much longer. It's too cold in here for the boys.

A fire would warm it up nicely. I saw some on the back porch."

He grinned at her. "Yes, ma'am."

"Okay then." She tightened her scarf. "Please let me know what your uncle says about the buildings. If there is anything I can do to change his mind, you know I'll do it."

He nodded but didn't say anything. There was a gleam in his eyes, as if he knew she was confused by him.

She stood over the boys. Tomas had kicked the blanket off his feet. She tucked him back in. "Do you want me to bring lunch after church tomorrow?"

The right corner of his mouth went up. "No. I promise I'll feed them."

"Of course. I could still bring out some lunch, and maybe I can go see the site of the old town?"

"Jackie, without talking to my uncle I can't promise you'll be able to have the buildings. He might still want me to take them down."

"I understand. But if I could at least see them and take some pictures for the records I've put together on their history."

"You know, they might not even be standing." He stuffed his hands in his jacket. "But if you're sure you want to go, we can drive out there in the afternoon."

"Thank you." She turned to leave, trying to walk calmly as if she wasn't running for her life, but the pounding of her heart could probably be heard across the room. "Bye, Ethan."

The teen glanced up from his phone. "Bye."

Max followed her out and stood at the edge of the porch, watching as she climbed into her car.

She started the engine but just sat there for a moment. Head bowed, she prayed. *God, this is the closest I've been to these buildings. It's been so heavy on my heart. Please open the Delgado family to seeing what I see.* Not understanding her feelings for Max, she didn't even know what to pray for when it came to him. She needed to stay focused on the buildings.

If she could make this work, this would be the year those buildings could be part of the Christmas celebration. The way her mother had envisioned it. Max's mother, too.

It was all written out in her mother's journals. The women had been working together against Max's father and her father's wishes. Now she was the one who had to make it right. Her father might grumble that he didn't want her to do this, but when he stood together with her sisters, he'd see it was all worth it.

She glanced in her rearview mirror as she drove off. Max stood alone.

Just like the day her father took her away from the dance. It had been total selfishness on her part. She'd rather have seen the hurt in Max's eyes than the hatred she'd known would have been there if she'd confessed to him the reason his mother lost control of the car.

Selfish coward.

How different would their lives have been if she'd listened to her father? It wouldn't have taken any time to put her toys away instead of leaving them in the car.

If her father, sisters and Max knew the truth, they would all hate her. She had destroyed two families. *Please, God, let me at least finish the dream our mothers started.*

She could never make it completely right, but if she preserved these buildings that meant so much to them, it would honor their memories.

Chapter Four

Standing up from working on the fence, Max tried to roll his shoulder, but the pain was too much. It was taking him longer to recover from broken bones than it had in the past. Age was not a bull rider's friend.

He went to his truck and dug around in his bag until he found the painkillers. Pills were not his first choice for controlling the pain. Too many cowboys started relying on them to live. Depending on anything but himself was a no go for him.

After throwing back three pills, he swallowed and glanced around the barn area for the boys. Ethan was standing with the two horses, but he didn't see Tomas or Isaac anywhere. He glanced at his watch and was surprised to see it was way past one o'clock. Jackie should have been here. She didn't seem like the kind that would be late.

"Ethan. Where are the boys? It's time to head back to the house."

"Yeah." He pointed to the barn. "They were in the old tac—"

A scream came from the loft area. BAM! Something hit hard.

"Tomas! Max!" Incoherent yelling from Isaac followed.

With Ethan right behind him, Max raced into the barn. Tomas was in the middle of the floor. Shattered pieces of wood surrounded the small body. He wasn't moving.

Falling to his knees beside the still figure, Max put his hand on the slight shoulder.

Tomas cried out. Okay. That meant he was breathing. That was good. Max said a silent prayer of gratitude. He was alive and conscious.

"Tomas. Where does it hurt?" He removed his work gloves and scanned the area for blood as he assessed the boy.

"The floor fell." Above them, Isaac's tear-stained face peered over the edge of the hole in the loft. Between panting and crying, it was tough to make sense of his words. "Is he dead?"

"No. He's going to be all right. Stay right where you are, Isaac. Don't move an inch." Supporting Tomas's neck, Max gently turned him, and for the second time in two days he prayed harder than he ever had.

All the color was gone from Tomas's face. "No blood." He pushed the boy's hair away from his eyes. "Where does it hurt?" Max knew the real danger could be impossible to see. With as much care as he could, he started running his hands over his brother's legs and arms.

Then he saw it.

"My—" the boy gave a deep sob "—my arm hurts."

"Yeah, I see that." The lower part of the boy's arm was bent at an unnatural angle. The skin wasn't broken, but it was evident that the bone wasn't so fortunate.

"Oh." Ethan gagged. His skin went a pasty white. He bent over, leaning on his knees. "His arm!"

"Ethan." Max stared into the teen's eyes, hoping to convey the importance of remaining calm. "I need you to get the first-aid kit under my back seat."

Ethan just stood there.

"Now."

Without a word, the kid ran from the barn.

"Tomas, look at me." Max cupped his little brother's face, taking in all the details. His eyes were clouded with pain, but otherwise looked good. "Does it hurt anywhere else?"

"My arm and it's hard…to breathe."

As if he had just realized his lungs weren't working, his dark eyes filled with panic.

"Tomas. Look at me. You just got the air knocked out of you. It happens to cowboys all the time. I need you to stay still. Let's take slow deep breaths together. Okay?" Max placed his hand on the narrow chest. "In, one…two… Out, one…two…"

Tomas nodded and closed his eyes. With his good arm, he reached out to Max as he turned his head against his older brother's thigh.

Max gently squeezed the small hand. He looked up at Isaac. "Listen to me. I don't want you to fall, too, so stay flat and scoot back. Away from the hole. Then don't move until Ethan or I can go up the ladder and help you down. Do you understand, Isaac?"

A few sobs echoed through the big barn. "Yes…sir. Are you sure… Tomas is okay?"

Ethan came running, the red bag tucked under his arm. He knelt on Tomas's other side. "I'm so sorry. I thought they would be fine in the barn. I'm so sorry."

"It's okay, Ethan. It's an old barn. I should have been

watching them better. I'm going to stabilize his arm. I need you to call 9-1-1."

Ethan's eyes widened. "It's that bad?"

Max took a deep breath. "He fell a good ways. I'm not sure if he lost consciousness. It's just a precaution."

Ethan placed the phone to his ear and started explaining their location and the accident.

"I'm going to get…to ride in an ambulance?" Tomas murmured.

A car pulled up outside. They couldn't be here already.

"Max?" Jackie called from outside. "Ethan?"

"Jackie's here." Ethan stated the obvious. He looked relieved to have another adult present. "Okay…Yes, ma'am," he said into the phone. He looked at Max. "They want me to stand at the road, so they know where we are."

"Good. Tell Jackie we're in here."

Before Ethan made it out the door, Jackie stood there.

"Max! What happened?" She hurried into the barn and bent over Tomas. She touched the boy's forehead gently. "Looks like you're having another adventure." She looked up at the new hole in the ceiling and stifled a gasp.

She quickly smiled. "Isaac, what in the world are you doing up in that old loft?" She glanced at Max, a question in her green eyes. "What can I do to help? I'm so sorry I'm late. I should have been here thirty minutes ago. Ethan's waiting for the ambulance?"

"Yes. Seems Tomas wanted to put a new escape route in." Max shifted Tomas slightly, moving him as little as possible. "I'm not sure if he was knocked out for a bit. If you would stay with him, I'll go up and get Isaac down. I don't want any more falling boys."

She took Tomas and frowned at the temporary splint. "I've got him. Be careful. If it gave way with the boys…"

With Tomas safe in Jackie's lap, Max went after Isaac. "I'm just going far enough up the ladder to get him."

He checked each wooden rung before putting any weight on it. They all seemed strong enough. When his head and shoulders emerged into the loft, he studied the area. Isaac clung to the edge of the jagged wood that had fallen out from under the boys. "Isaac. I'm right behind you. I want you to stay on your belly, but push back so I can touch your ankle."

"I'm scared."

"I know. That's why I'm here. Together we're going to get you down. I just need you to scoot backward."

Isaac didn't move.

Max took a deep breath. He really didn't want to test the integrity of the loft floor with his weight. But how was he going to get Isaac to move toward him?

"Isaac." Jackie's voice sounded free of all his frustration. "Max needs you to wiggle over to him, so he can get you down. Do you know how to wiggle like a worm?"

He nodded and slowly squirmed a couple inches.

"Good job, Isaac."

Wood creaked. Isaac cried out and froze. Max reached as far as he could, but he wasn't close enough yet. Isaac covered his head with his hands and let out a deep sob.

Maybe Max should have called for the fire truck, too. "Isaac, don't stop now. Look, I almost have you."

The five-year-old twisted around. His small face was full of trust. Trust Max didn't deserve. He forced a smile he didn't feel. "Come on, we got this."

"Be a slow wiggling worm, Isaac," Jackie encouraged from the barn floor.

With a barely there nod, Isaac started scooting again. Max's hands made contact. Briefly he closed his eyes and breathed again. *Thank You, God.* "I got you, Isaac. Just a little farther."

He got close enough that Max could pull him into his arms. Small hands clung to him as Isaac cried against his neck. Max pressed his cheek against the soft hair. "Shh. It's okay."

"I'm so sorry." His words were spread between sobs. "Is Tomas okay?"

"Yeah. I'm going to put you on my back, and I need you to hang on tight." Supporting his bottom, Max moved Isaac to his back. His shoulder screamed in protest, but he gritted his teeth. Rung by painful rung, they got to the ground. Isaac slid off, running to his brother.

Ethan sprinted into the barn. "They're here." He looked behind him and shouted, "He's in here."

Three EMTs entered the barn. One carried a board that Max had seen too many times in the arena. Fear rose in him. He tried to swallow the feeling that he had let them down. Twice.

Everything became a blur at that point. Isaac was back in his arms. Scared.

"Brenda, this is Tomas. He fell from the loft." Of course, Jackie would know the EMTs.

The dark-haired woman was petite but strong-looking. The giant man from the feed store, Jim, was gentle as he strapped Tomas to the board. Another young man he didn't recognize quietly helped.

Jim started telling the boys about the puppies as Brenda checked Tomas. She looked at Max. "Do you know if he lost consciousness?"

"I'm not sure. I heard him fall." He was never going to forget the sound of the wood splitting and the body of his little brother hitting the ground.

"You're his guardian?"

"Yes. I'm his brother." He didn't deserve to be. He pulled Isaac closer and kissed the top of his head as he kept his gaze on Tomas. He looked so small on the stretcher.

"You can ride with us." She turned to Jackie. "You have the other two boys?"

She nodded. "Yes."

Brenda nodded to the two men, and they took Tomas to the ambulance.

"I want to go with him!" Isaac pushed away from Max.

Jackie took Isaac before he could run after his brother. "We'll let them take Tomas so they can make sure he's good." She looked at Max. "Do you want me to bring Ethan and Isaac to the hospital or stay here with them?"

He had never been in this kind of situation. He hated not knowing what to do.

Isaac strained against her hold. "I want Tomas!"

Jackie pulled him closer as they all walked to the ambulance. "We'll be right behind them in my car." She looked at Max. "Is that okay?"

Max stayed as close as he could to Tomas. "Okay."

"I want to go with him." Isaac reached for his brother.

Brenda smiled at him. "We're going to take him to Kerrville. The doctors will want to take a couple of pictures of your brother's insides to make sure he's all good."

Jackie grabbed Max's hand with her free one. Her warmth calmed him for a moment. "I'll have the boys there. We'll get through this." She stepped back. "Come on, Ethan. Let's get in my car."

For the first time in his life, Max climbed into the ambulance, rather than being carried in on the stretcher. This would be so much easier to handle if he was the one hurt. He closed his eyes for a moment and thanked God that Jackie had arrived.

Jackie shifted Isaac to her other shoulder. The green vinyl chairs in the waiting room were not designed for comfort. In his sleep, the five-year-old had started sucking his thumb. She rested her cheek against his soft hair. The unfairness of life just ate at her sometimes.

Ethan gave another heavy sigh and began pacing for the fourth time. Pastor Levi came back into the waiting area and sat down next to her. He took a cup from the drink carrier on his knees and pulled some snacks out of his coat pocket. "Here's your coffee."

"Thank you so much. You really don't have to stay. I'm sure Max will be out soon."

"I'm good." He looked at the restless teen. "Ethan, I got you a Dr. Pepper. Do you want an apple or some cheese sticks?"

The teen sat down next to the pastor and took the apple. "Thanks. Are they ever going to tell us anything?"

"Waiting is the hard part. Just have faith that they're doing everything they can to make sure he's healthy." He turned back to Jackie. "Here, let me take Isaac so you can properly savor that coffee." He gently took the boy from her arms.

It surprised her how empty they suddenly felt. She had only known the little boy for two days, and he wasn't even related to her.

Being without mothers and feeling alone might be the connection. She shouldn't analyze it too deeply. Taking a slow sip, she let the warm liquid slide down her throat. It was creamy and sweet, just the way she liked it. "Does this have vanilla in it?"

"Yeah. It's the only way Lorrie Ann drinks her coffee," he said, referring to his wife.

"How are she and the baby doing?" She needed something to focus on other than Max and his brothers.

"Good. He's not sleeping through the night yet, but we're getting closer."

"I'll stop by tomorrow and give her a chance to take a nap. Playing with babies is one of my specialties." She leaned over and brushed a curl back from Isaac's sweet face. It seemed she would always be the aunt or the friend, never the mom.

The double doors opened, and Max stepped through, moving to the side as a nurse pushed Tomas in a small wheelchair. A camouflage cast extended from Tomas's knuckles to his elbow.

Ethan was first at the boy's side. "He's okay?" He was looking at Max as he sat on his haunches in front of the wheelchair.

Max squeezed his shoulder. "Yeah. Other than a broken arm and a story he'll get to tell his friends."

"The nurse said I was real brave. They said my brain didn't get scrambled, but I'm going to be sore for the next few days."

Jackie heard a whimper behind her. She turned and saw Isaac with tears in his eyes.

She took him from Pastor Levi and held him close. He pressed his face into her hair. "He can't walk? His legs don't work?"

Stroking his soft hair, she shook her head. "He's okay.

Everyone has to be in a wheelchair when they leave the hospital." She put him down.

"Oh." He walked to his brother. "Tomas, you're okay?"

"Look at my cast." He held his arm up. "They let me pick the color. It's camouflaged. It's cool, right?"

The nurse smiled. "I would suggest no more exploring old buildings, though."

Jackie patted Ethan's shoulder. "Y'all ready to go home?"

Max sighed. "I know I am."

Pastor Levi stood next to Jackie. "Do you want to pray before you leave?"

With a scowl on his face, Isaac looked between Pastor Levi and Jackie. "I thought God lived in church. Why would we pray here?"

Ethan rolled his eyes. "Don't be so lame."

"Ethan." Max glared at the teen.

Pastor Levi glanced at Max. "Sorry. If you don't—"

Max shook his head. "No. I'd appreciate the prayer." He ruffled Tomas's hair. "We can talk to God anytime. He's everywhere."

"That's true." The pastor knelt in front of Tomas. "Some people act like God only lives at the church, but God is always with us. Do you want to pray now with your family?"

Tomas looked up at Max, uncertainty in his eyes.

With a nod, Max put his hand on Tomas's shoulder. Jackie reached for Max's free hand. The little group formed a circle.

John Levi's soothing voice talked of peace and healing, faith and love. Prayer always moved Jackie, but this circle of a broken family touched her heart in ways that made her want to cry.

When Pastor Levi finished, he patted Max on the shoulder. The grimace of pain was slight, but Jackie saw it. It seemed Tomas wasn't the only one hurt.

"Hope to see you in church. The door is always open, and we have a good youth program for the boys. They could meet kids their age."

Max nodded, his smile tight. "Thanks. We'll see how the week goes."

Jackie focused on the pastor. For some reason, she couldn't look at Max right now. "Tell Lorrie Ann hi for me. Let her know I'll stop by Monday at noon." She felt raw and exposed. She'd been late to Max's place this afternoon because she could find neither her keys nor some of the paperwork she wanted to show him. She'd been distracted and let her anxiety mess with her mind and schedule. When things were out of order, people got hurt. This time it had been an innocent little boy.

Part of her knew it wasn't rational to think this was her fault, but if she'd gone out to the ranch as arranged, this wouldn't have happened.

She pulled her car around to the double doors and Ethan climbed into the back seat. Max put Isaac down and lifted Tomas from his wheelchair. Taking the younger brother's hand, Jackie led him to the other side and got him buckled in.

Once everyone was in, she pulled out and headed back to Clear Water. "Who's hungry?"

"Me!" Tomas was the first to speak up. "Max said if I did good I could get ice cream."

"Ice cream. Isn't it kind of cold for that?" Ethan grumbled from the back.

"Never. I want one, too." Isaac waved his arms.

She looked at Max. He just shrugged and smiled at her. "I did promise him ice cream, and he was a champ."

"Okay, will Dairy Queen work? We could get a chocolate-dipped cone." She glanced at Ethan. "What about you, Ethan? Do you like Dairy Queen?"

"Never eaten there."

"What!" She shook her head as she turned at the light. "How can you call yourself a Texan and not have eaten at Dairy Queen? I'm afraid to ask about Whataburger."

Ethan lifted one eyebrow and tilted his head as if she spoke an alien language. "You know I live in Chicago."

"Doesn't matter. You were born in Texas, right?"

"Yeah?"

She grinned at him. "Your family has been part of Texas before it was even Texas. You're a Texan no matter where you live. Say no more. We will fix this horrible wrong." She glanced over at Max. "How could you let this happen?"

He chuckled. "Hey, I'm here now and ready to right this wrong."

"What's Water Burger?" Tomas asked.

"Sounds kind of gross." Isaac wrinkled his nose.

"What. A. Burger. But I think just about everybody called it Water Burger at one point in their life." Max laughed. "So, as your older brother, I say we start with the best burgers in the country, then stop at Dairy Queen for a chocolate-dipped cone."

"Yay!" The young brothers cheered at the same time.

Once they got their orange-striped bags and cups, they headed to Dairy Queen.

"Are we going to the old buildings when we get back?" Ethan popped a couple of fries into his mouth. "What are we going to do with Double Trouble here? We can't get any work done if they're going to be getting lost or hurt every time we turn our backs on them. You'll never be able to teach me to ride."

"We'll work something out." Max didn't look like he believed his own statement.

Isaac slurped his soda. "We promise to be good. We won't climb into the loft again."

"Or disappear," Tomas added.

Max tilted his head back and rubbed his temples. Jackie thought about offering to help, but her survival instinct screamed no. The more she hung out with Max and his brothers, the easier it would be to forget all the reasons she needed to keep her distance. Her heart couldn't take any more hurt.

She needed to focus on the buildings and not those two lost little boys. Out of the corner of her eye, she saw Max tapping his fingers against his thigh. In the rear-view mirror, Ethan had finished his ice cream and was now staring out the window. Make that four lost boys. Well, Max wasn't a boy, but he might be the most lost.

"Jackie? Are you going to turn?"

The old, worn entry was already there. "Sorry!" Her foot hit the brake and the Tahoe rolled past the driveway. Coming to a stop, she checked behind them before slipping into Reverse to be able to turn into the property. This was what happened when she got distracted. "I'm so sorry."

"Where were you?"

"She's in the car, Max!" The boys giggled and Ethan rolled his eyes, but his smile said he wasn't as cynical as he pretended.

She felt Max's gaze on her as she fixated on the road. She needed to avoid looking at him.

"Jackie."

She let the silence sit between them. She would pretend she didn't hear him.

He wasn't taking the hint. "Jackie, I have an idea."

Her heart did a double take. She dodged a hole in the road.

"The boys need more supervision, and I have work I need to get done." He moved his hand until it rested on the back of her seat, almost touching her. "The boys know you and like you."

"We do!" The youngest brothers yelled in stereo.

"Dorks." Ethan shook his head.

Pulling up to the house, she saw Sammi's truck was parked behind a white work van. Great opportunity to change the subject and derail Max's train of thought before he went where she was afraid of going. "Looks like you might have lights. Maybe you'll finally be able to move in to your house."

Putting the car in Park and cutting the engine, she went to open the door. She needed to escape.

"Jackie, wait a minute."

She closed her eyes.

"Is there a way that you could help me out with the boys until their aunt comes and gets them?" His warm hand brushed her shoulder. "She's trying to get here sooner to take the boys. Maybe this weekend. But until then I really need some help."

She shook her head. "I can't, Max. I'm sorry."

"We don't want to leave," said Tomas, while Isaac spoke on top of him, "I want to stay here with you." Then they both nodded and added, "We'll be good, Max."

"I thought we were going to stay together through Christmas?" Ethan leaned forward to push the seat down. "Never mind. It doesn't matter. Whatever. Can we get out, or are we going to sit here all day?"

Jackie opened her door. "Sammi's truck is here, and she has been known to work wonders. Let's get the boys inside and see if you have lights and heat." As she helped Isaac out of his seat belt, the defeat and sadness in all three boys tore at her heart. They needed family, and Max was being too selfish to see it. She glanced across to the opposite door where Max was gently helping Tomas.

He needed to shave, and his hair was a mess. She bit the inside of her cheek to stop the words she'd regret. Isaac clung to her neck before she could put him on the ground. Ethan shoved the seat forward and climbed out. After slamming the door, he brushed past her and stomped up the sidewalk to the front porch.

"Ethan." Max's voice was low, but it had a hard edge to it. "You need to apologize to Jackie. That was rude."

"Sor-ry." The two syllables came through clenched teeth. Ethan turned to Max. "I thought we were staying together through Christmas. I should have known you'd end up ditching us. Like everyone else."

"Ethan, this has nothing to do with that. I'm not sure I'm able to keep the boys safe. The sooner they get settled in their real life, the better."

Ethan took a step toward Max. "So, the whole brother-bonding thing was a lie? Why did you even bring us out here?" He blinked, then wiped his face. It was heartbreaking to watch the teen fight back the tears. When he raised his eyes again, the I-don't-care look had returned. His complexion was lighter than Max's and the boys', but the stubborn jaw and the cut of the features were the same.

"I do want to get to know you and the boys. That wasn't—"

"Save it for someone who cares. I just don't understand why you bothered to drive us all down here. Is it the money?" He snarled his lips and crossed his arms, pulling into himself. "My stepbrothers said I'm worth a lot of money now that my father's dead."

Max took a step toward the angry teen, but Ethan stepped back, chin up. "Whatever. I don't care. I'll be eighteen in less than two years, and I can do whatever I want with it."

"First of all, I walked away from our father's money years ago. I couldn't care less about that. Second, I do want us to get to know each other and be there for each other as brothers. You want the truth? I'm in over my head. I've had y'all for two days, and they've gotten lost, one's broken an arm and you've barely said more than a few words. I don't know what I'm doing, and I'm afraid the three of you are going to pay the price of my ignorance. Plus, you don't get access to your inheritance until you're twenty-five."

"Twenty-five! That's like a hundred years from now! That's not fair." Ethan's breathing became heavier. "And now that we caused a little trouble, you're going to give up and throw us away like Dad did?" He couldn't stop the tears from falling this time, but his lips and jaw were still unforgiving.

Jackie pulled Tomas closer to her. He had started crying, too. A frigid gust blew dead leaves across the sidewalk.

Isaac stood beside her, his small hand in hers. It was trembling. His black lashes were wet. "I'm sorry, Max. If you let us stay, I promise we'll be good."

Jackie swallowed the reassuring words that rose to her lips. She couldn't make any promises. It was Max's call. His gaze was fixed on her like she was some sort of life preserver.

He looked as lost as his brothers, but he was the adult here. He needed to make this right for them. It wasn't her place. Besides, she already had enough keeping her own family safe and happy.

The screen door opened, and Sammi emerged from the house followed by Eddie Walters.

Jackie stepped forward. "Good to see you here, Eddie. This is Max. Max, this is Edward Walters. Hopefully, he'll tell us your house is ready to move in to."

He shook Max's hand and laughed. "Move-in ready might be a little optimistic, but the electricity is working, and the safety hazards have been fixed. It's safer than the barn, from what I hear."

"Yeah, the place needs some work." Max crammed his fists into his pockets. "Would you have time to look at the rest of the buildings? I'd like to make sure all the wiring is sound before we burn something down. I've been given orders to get it ready for market."

Eddie narrowed his eyes. "This place has been in your family before we were even Texas. Y'all selling out now? Not to some developers I hope."

"My uncle's head of the family holdings now. He's making the decisions. Can you do the work, or should I call someone from Kerrville?"

"I can come out after Thanksgiving. How many buildings are you talking about?"

"There are three large barns, a couple of smaller homes and I think there are two bunkhouses. Would you be able to check them all out to make sure they're safe for now, and see which ones we can get running again and which ones need to come down?"

"Sure. Sounds like a big job. I have a couple of local boys that can help. What about the old town? Want me to inspect those?"

"Yeah, I think that would be a good idea. We can make a better decision about them."

Jackie gasped. "Did your uncle change his mind about tearing them down?"

"No, but I'm still talking to him." He wouldn't look at her.

Did she dare to hope?

Eddie pulled up the hood of his jacket. "I'll talk to you later, Delgado. Call me, and we'll go over details."

Without a backward glance, the electrician made for his van.

Sammi opened the front door. "Come on, guys. It's warm in here."

They gathered in the living room. A massive fire was popping in the fireplace.

Sammi rubbed her hands in front of the flames. "I think this might end up being the coldest Thanksgiving on record." She turned to Max. "I still say y'all should join us."

Max shook his head. "We're good."

Jackie took a deep breath. The idea of them alone with no big meal when her family had more than they needed ate at her. She would probably regret this, but if she didn't say anything the guilt would ruin her Thanksgiving. "Really, you and the boys should join us. One of my aunts brings in some military personnel that are away from home, so we'll have more than family there. The four of you'll blend right in. And the boys'll have fun."

He held her gaze for a moment. Despite the cold, she felt her neck getting warm. She looked at the fire. "There'll be tons of food. And pies. All sorts of pies."

"Can we go?" Tomas cradled his arm.

"Please? I want to go." Isaac nodded.

Max looked about as happy as someone waving a white flag. "What time should we be there?"

Sammi smiled. "Anytime between one and two. Happy y'all are joining us." She made her way to the door. "I'm going home. You coming, Jackie?"

"Yeah. I'll be right behind you." She knelt in front of Tomas. "You be careful. No more climbing, okay?"

"Yes, ma'am."

She hugged him, then Isaac.

Max stood at the door. "Thank you for your help today. I don't know—"

"No problem. I just wish I'd gotten here when I'd planned. Then it wouldn't have happened at all." She knew it wasn't her fault, but still, if she hadn't been afraid of seeing Max again she would have been out here before Tomas fell. "You're right about one thing. You do need help with the boys if you're going to be doing ranch work. Ethan is old enough to help you, but they're too young. I'll ask my sister Danica for some names of babysitters she uses for her daughters." Okay, she needed to leave now. "Bye." Before she turned to go, she made the mistake of looking at Max.

The space between his eyes formed a V. She wanted to hug him, too, but she knew that was a line she couldn't cross. With one last obligatory smile, she forced herself out the door.

As soon as she stepped outside, freezing rain pelted her face. The sidewalk was already slick.

Max stood on the edge of the porch. "Are you sure it's safe to drive? Do you want me to follow you? Maybe you should call your dad."

She waved. "I'm a big girl. I've driven in worse." For her own sanity, she needed to leave. If she wasn't careful her heart was going to get crushed. She wasn't sure if it would be losing the buildings forever or losing Max again that would be worse.

In the car, she turned on the heat while she sent a text to her father, letting him know she was heading home and traveling slow.

He replied right away, telling her to be careful. She stared at the phone. Now would be a good time to let him know who was coming for dinner. No, she needed to tell him face-to-face. As she tossed the phone back into her bag, she could imagine her sisters making chicken noises.

Releasing the brake, she sat for a bit, looking down the long curving ranch road. Max would be at the Bergmann Thanksgiving dinner. Her father was going to have a fit. And not just her father. Her aunts, cousins… the whole lot would think she'd lost her mind and forgotten their history.

Chapter Five

Surrounded by her sisters, Jackie was in her happy zone. She pulled the pecan pies out of Danica's new oven, bumping into Nikki as she backed up. "Sorry."

After years away in the navy, her oldest sister, Nikki, was living in Clear Water again and to everyone's surprise married to Adrian De La Cruz. She was a wonderful stepmother to his daughter, Mia. Now they were expecting their first child and building a family of their own.

Nikki laughed. "No worries. I have no sense of space with this huge basketball strapped to my middle." She rubbed her expanding tummy. "There's no way I'm going to last another two months. I told Adrian the doctor needed to look at his little chart again."

Danica slid a green bean casserole into the oven. "You're not that big. Be thankful it's not twins. By my last trimester, everyone was avoiding me."

"I wish people would leave me alone. Between Adrian, his family and Daddy, you'd think no woman had ever had a child before. Even Mia has conspired against me and reports to her father if she thinks I'm overdoing it. I thought we had a special bond past the whole stepmom vs. stepdaughter thing."

"You're a great stepmother. She loves you and the whole family is excited about the baby. The doctor did tell you to be careful and take it easy." Jackie really wanted to tell her sisters they had no right to ever complain about being wives and mothers. But it might make her sound petty. Instead, she smiled. "Can't believe we're finally adding a boy to the family."

"Mia's at her grandparents, so Adrian wanted me to wait for him to finish at the ranch. He's really getting ridiculous. I had to promise to sit and not do anything if I wanted to come over without him." Nikki perched on a stool and sighed. "I flew into war zones, but apparently I can't handle household chores." She looked over at Danica, now at the sink rinsing mixing bowls. "Was Daddy this bad with you?"

"Yes." Danica glanced over her shoulder at Jackie. "Speaking of Daddy, how did he take the news that Max was coming for dinner?"

Jackie loved hanging out with her sisters, and now that Nikki was back in town and happy, her family felt complete. Well, as complete as you can feel when you were missing the pin that held everyone together. She mashed the potatoes a bit harder than needed.

"Jacqueline Bergmann! You haven't told him, have you?" Danica faced her, hands on hips. "They'll be here in a few hours. Do you think it's wise—or even fair—for them to walk in and surprise Dad? You need to tell him and explain. Before *they* get here! I don't want drama at my first Thanksgiving in my new home!"

"I'm going to tell him. With the pies and—"

"You've had plenty of time."

"Dad's not here. I don't even know where he is."

Jackie started pulling fresh fruit out of the refrigerator. "Have I told you how much I love these appliances? That husband of yours did a great job."

"Reid told me you gave him a list and he bought them." Danica stood on the other side of the large island, one eyebrow lifted. Jackie knew that look. Danica wasn't going to let her ignore the question.

"Not answering the question won't make it go away," Nikki chimed in. "Why haven't you told Dad?"

Jackie shrugged. Not a single truthful answer came to mind. Not one that she was willing to share, anyway. The idea of having Max and her father in the same room made her much more nervous than it should have. She loved her sisters, but sometimes they were too bossy.

"It's no big deal. There'll be so many people here, Daddy might not even notice a few more guests."

"How are *you* with him being here?" Danica asked.

Jackie refused to look at her twin. She might see too much. "Me? I'm fine." She heard her voice go up. She cleared her throat. "I have no feelings one way or the other."

Now it was Nikki's turn to raise her brows.

"Anyway, Sammi invited them first. She should tell Daddy." She always avoided telling her father anything that might upset him. She just wanted him happy. "Where is he?"

"He went with Sonia to the Ortegas' family lunch. Then they're coming over here."

That got her attention. Her father had never brought a lady friend to Thanksgiving before. He never had a lady friend to bring, not since Sammi's mom walked out on them. "Daddy's bringing Sonia to our family Thanksgiving? Like a date? Are they dating?"

Nikki shrugged. "I don't know. He just said that,

since we weren't doing dinner at his house, he was going to go with her to her family thing, then head over here."

Danica threw the washrag on the counter. "So, this means they're officially dating, right? Going to family events is a pretty big deal. He really needs to be careful with her. You know she has a rough past."

Pausing in cutting a pineapple, Jackie looked at her sisters. It was common knowledge that Sonia was a recovering alcoholic. "How do we feel about this?"

Nikki leaned on the counter. "I heard she's been sober for four or five years now."

"Yeah, but—" Danica clapped her hand over her mouth and dashed from the kitchen.

Nikki watched her go, then turned back to Jackie. "She looked a little green, and I don't think it has anything to do with Daddy dating Sonia."

"I noticed she hasn't been eating much this last week. And she's been late to work twice. Do you think she's pregnant?"

"This is the second time I've seen her dash to the bathroom. And she's been back together with Reid for almost a year now." Nikki rubbed her belly. "It wouldn't surprise me."

"My sisters are married and expanding the family, and I can't even get a date."

Sammi stomped the mud off her boots at the back door. "I'm not married or even dating. Not that I want to. I think we might be better off."

Returning to the kitchen, Danica walked straight to the sink and washed her hands, but before anyone could answer, the back door opened again and their father was standing in the doorway. His gaze swept the room. Concern was etched into every line on his stern face. "What's wrong?"

"We're okay. We were just having a sister moment."

He shook his head. Years of raising four girls alone had taught him to take mood swings in stride.

Danica tossed her braid over her shoulder. "Jackie does have something to tell you, though."

"Thanks, sis." Jackie narrowed her eyes, making sure Danica knew how she felt about being shoved out of the protective circle.

Turning back to her father, she put her best smile on. "Daddy, since we're having our first Thanksgiving here, and we've invited all of Adrian's family and the ranch hands Reid works with and the military folks, I figured we should open our doors to anyone that needed a place to give thanks and eat." She finally took a breath.

"Girl, you're rambling." He set his jaw. "Of course, we've always opened the door to anyone in need. What's your point?"

"Yes." She looked at her sisters. "See, we agree."

"Who did you invite?" Full-on suspense was boiling over with each word. "Jacqueline?"

With a deep breath, she made her smile bigger. "Max Delgado and his brothers have nowhere to go. The boys are only five and six and they just lost their parents. No one should spend their first holiday without their parents alone, right?"

"You invited Frankie Delgado's sons to my house for Thanksgiving? Rigo Delgado's nephews will be at my table?"

"Well, technically it's Danica's house. And Frankie and his wife were killed in a boating accident. Now those two little boys don't have anywhere to experience a real Thanksgiving. It's the right thing to do. That's what you taught us."

Before her father could reply, the back door opened

and Joaquin came in, carrying a couple of white boxes. Jackie held her breath. How would Joaquin feel about Max and the boys being here? They never talked about his biological father, Rigo Delgado.

The man had lied to Joaquin's mother and then abandoned her when she became pregnant with Joaquin. Feeling bad for the boy, her father had taken him in, later offering him a job. Over the years Joaquin had become family.

"Hey, guys. I brought the rest of the table and chairs." He was followed by a petite dark-haired woman. "And I found this lady at the gate." He smiled at Sonia, who was carrying more white pastry boxes with her bakery's logo.

It was strange to watch her father rush over to Sonia and take her burden. "I'm so sorry. I forgot you don't have the code. Remind me to give it to you."

Sonia looked up at him with absolute love in her eyes. Unease settled in Jackie's stomach. She was not the kind of woman she would have chosen for her dad. She seemed nice enough, but his second wife had hurt him beyond repair. Jackie didn't want to see him taken advantage of by another woman.

Sammi perched on the granite counter and bit into an apple. "Where do you want us to set up?"

Danica gripped the edge of the island, her head down. "The red barn. Reid and the guys cleaned it out. They have the heaters going, so it should be warm enough."

Sammi hopped down. "Come on, guys. Let's get those tables set up. When will Reid be back?"

"He should be back in about an hour. He'll have some of the cowboys with him."

Sammi nodded and headed out the door, Joaquin close behind.

Her father pegged Jackie with a hard look. "Have you told Joaquin?"

The young cowboy stopped and cocked his head to the side. "Told Joaquin what?"

"It's really no big deal." She smiled at Joaquin. *Yeah, right. Then why is my stomach in a knot?*

After a moment of silence, his gaze darted around the room. "Did I do something wrong?"

Jackie shook her head. "No. There's someone coming to dinner that… Well, we don't want you to be surprised or anything."

"Okay." He raised an eyebrow. "And this mystery person is…"

"Max Delgado and his brothers."

Sonia sucked in her breath. "How can you have a Delgado here after the way Rigo Delgado treated Mercedes?"

Jackie had forgotten that Sonia and Mercedes, Joaquin's mother, were best friends. "If you don't want him here, I'll call him and—"

"No." Joaquin smiled at Sonia. "Thank you for your loyalty to my mom. But Max is not Rigo. He can't be held accountable for what his uncle and grandfather did."

Sammi wrapped her hand around his upper arm. "I don't think Max even knows about your mother."

Joaquin snorted. "I'm not sure if the other Delgados not knowing about me makes me feel better or worse. Either way, I'd love to meet him. He really knows how to ride a bull, and it'll be great to talk shop."

Her father headed for the door. "If that's settled, we have tables to set up."

Her married sisters went back to talking about their husbands and kids as they chopped, mixed and basted.

The comforting hum of familiar conversations surrounded her.

Jackie's heart went a little heavy. This chatter had never made her sad before. Now she was wondering if she would ever have her own family.

Chapter Six

Max parked his pickup behind a long line of other trucks in front of the cozy ranch house. "Okay, boys. We're guests, so use your best manners. Say please and thank you and offer to help whenever you can. Got it?"

Ethan slumped against the seat. "What? You afraid we're going to embarrass you?"

Max twisted to face his brother sitting next to him. "Ethan, look at me." He waited for the teen to comply. "There is nothing you could do that would make me embarrassed to call you my brother, but I'm a little nervous going into a strange group of people. So, I was reminding us all to be grateful and polite, understand?"

The teen nodded, then went back to staring out the window. "I know how to act. Not sure why we're here. If the town's any indication, no one wants us." He looked at Max. "What's up between you and Jackie? Were you a thing back in the day?"

Max gripped the steering wheel. He didn't want to talk about Jackie. "We are here because we were invited and it will be good for us to meet people." He lifted his hands in the air. "We just need to let them know that we come in peace."

Ethan rolled his eyes. "You're so lame."

Isaac had his seat belt off already. The boys were excited and ready to meet people. Ethan hadn't moved.

Max placed his hand on the teen's shoulder. "Come on, buddy. It's Thanksgiving. Everyone's happy."

"That's not how these things go down in my experience."

Anger for his father flared, but he swallowed the bile and relaxed his jaw. Ethan didn't need his anger. "I don't have a lot of good family experiences, either, but the boys are excited. We're the older brothers. We want them to have better memories than we had, don't we? I'm trying hard to make this work for all of us."

Ethan tilted his head back and studied the roof of the truck. "My stomach hurts. Can I just stay in the truck? I can lay down in the back bench seat."

"No. My guess is that you're anxious, which is fine. But I want you to think how disappointed Tomas and Isaac would be if you weren't there. I'd miss you, too. This is our first opportunity to have a real family holiday together. We haven't had any of those." He struggled with the words. It was so much easier to deal with bulls instead of people. People who he could damage with the wrong words. "Listen, Ethan. When our father sent me away, I was angry. I hated him. I resented your mother… and you. The cute little boy who replaced me. We both know it wasn't your fault, just like it's not their fault that our father stopped spending time with you when they came along. I haven't been here for you. I've been a lousy brother. This is a chance for us to change that."

"Why are you even trying? Isn't the plan to get rid of us as soon as you can?"

"I've thought of myself as not having family, but I do. I have you and…" He glanced at the two small boys who looked like him. "Those guys need us. I think we need them, too. Just because we won't be living together doesn't mean we can't be there for each other. This can be the start of new traditions. You have my number now. Call me whenever you need me. I'll answer, every time. We are family, and we can start acting like it even when we aren't in the same house."

The boys had climbed to the top of the truck's deer guard and were grinning at them through the windshield. Max shook his head. "Those two make smiling easy."

Ethan made a sound that could have been a chuckle. "They're so goofy."

"Come on. We can't let them down. They have a chance of having better memories than we had. We need you to make this new family. You with us?"

"Sure." Ethan opened the door and jumped to the ground.

As Max went around to the front of the truck, Jackie stepped out onto the large covered porch. She wore a green scarf tied around her neck, making her piled-up red hair look even richer. Max jerked his gaze from the loose curls brushing her cheek. He needed something—anything—else to look at before his wayward brain took him places he couldn't go.

"Hi, Max. Ethan!" With the warmest smile, she knelt in front of his little brothers. "And my two favorite men are here." She opened her arms, and they rushed her. Laughing, she caught her balance. "You're so strong, you almost knocked me over!"

The boys giggled, and Max caught Ethan with a slight smile. Maybe coming to the Bergmanns' hadn't been a mistake.

She stood and smiled. "Welcome and happy Thanksgiving. We're gathering at the barn to eat. Tons of room." She looked down at the boys. "And heaters. I don't remember it ever being this cold in November. Last year we were wearing shorts and going to the river."

They all followed her as she led them past the house and a grove of old pecan trees to a large red barn.

It was straight off a postcard. Bales of hay and bunches of fall leaves were stacked outside, while evergreen swags with red ribbons adorned the fence. White Christmas lights twinkled from the trees and edged the barn. A large palomino and a small pony stretched out their necks, wanting attention.

Isaac ran to the little one. "Look, Max. It's just our size."

Rubbing his head, Max had to laugh.

Jackie pushed open the sliding door and stepped aside. "Almost everyone's here. We don't stand on ceremony, so make yourself at home." An extensive brick walkway was lined with empty stalls. Several tables pushed together in the center were covered with more fall colors, while cut-glass goblets sparkled in the lights strung across the ceiling. It looked like a photo shoot staged for some high-end magazine.

Jackie pointed to a table against what looked to be a tack room. "Drinks are over there, and we have finger foods until the main course comes out." She looked at the boys. "Want something to eat?"

The boys nodded eagerly. Their small plates laden, Jackie moved them through the crowd, introducing them to more people than Max could remember. Everyone was pleasant, and the boys got a great deal of attention. The smell of hay and leather gave Max a familiar sense of comfort. Almost as though it was a place he could belong.

There had to be over thirty people here. Most of the crowd seemed to belong to the oldest sister, Nikki, and her husband, Adrian. Sammi came in carrying trays of food and being followed by a cowboy.

Jackie laid her hand on Max's upper arm, casually, as though she didn't even notice she was touching him. "This is Joaquin… Villarreal."

The cowboy looked familiar, but Max couldn't place him. "Good to meet you. Have we met before?"

Joaquin laughed. "Yeah. At a couple of rodeos. I'm pretty sure you wouldn't remember me." He shrugged and smiled. "It was just in passing. I've followed your career."

Jackie and Sammi were throwing silent messages back and forth.

Joaquin rolled his eyes, then turned back to Max. "Ignore the sisters. How's the head and shoulder? I saw that last ride."

"Fine. Part of the game. I plan to get to the finals, but I need to get in some practice. Jackie and Sammi said you ride. Would you be interested in joining me? Some spotters would be good."

"Me?" A startled expression flashed on his face then was gone. He nodded. "Sure, that would be great." He rubbed his chin, glancing at Sammi before looking back at Max. "I have a question. You don't have to answer if you don't want to. Your family's from Clear Water and Dallas, but you're listed as coming from Port Del Mar."

Jackie raised an eyebrow at him. "Really? Why?"

He shrugged, wanting to play it off as no big deal. "I was mad at the Delgados, so I claimed my mother's hometown as mine. It was just an immature rub at my father." He snorted. "Not that he cared."

"Aunt Jackie!" Two identical girls with red curly hair

ran over and jumped into Jackie's arms. "We went to see Mia's new horse."

The girls, who were about the same size as his brothers, looked so much like Jackie they could be her daughters. The boys stepped back and stared, openmouthed.

Jackie released them. "Suzie and Lizzy, these are the boys I was telling you about, Tomas and Isaac. Boys, these are my nieces."

With warm smiles, the sisters greeted the boys. "Aunt Jackie, can we show them the kittens?"

"Yes, if you promise to be gentle and speak softly."

"Yes, ma'am." They turned to Isaac and Tomas. "Do you want to see the kittens? They're in the last stall."

Both boys looked up at Max. "Fine, but be sure to stay in the barn." Almost before he had finished speaking, the girls had led the boys off.

Jackie smiled. "They'll be fine."

Ethan was staring across the room.

Max turned to see what had the teen's attention. "That's Kelsey, right? From the restaurant?"

His brother grunted. "Was that her name? I don't remember."

"Right."

Jackie touched Ethan's arm. "Do you want to go talk to her?"

"No. It's all right." His gaze darted around the barn. "Where do the kids have to sit?"

"Here, at the table."

Ethan looked at her if she was crazy. "With the grown-ups?"

"Yes. We sit together as a family. That's why we moved it out here. More room for everyone."

"I've never got to sit at the big table."

"Then welcome." She interlocked her arm around

Ethan's. "I know you met Kelsey and her mother already, but let's go talk to the other Pryces. They have a son about your age."

The teen didn't look sure.

"There are some other high schoolers over there, too. Kelsey keeps looking this way. It would be rude for you not to go over there."

Max elbowed him. "We came to talk to people. Go talk."

He watched as his brother joined the other teens. Another group laughed, and small clusters of people stood around chatting.

Isaac and Tomas came running back and grabbed his hands. "You have to see the kittens. They hissed at us. Can we have one?"

"I see a trend here. We don't know if Vanessa will let you get the puppies yet, so let's not add cats to the list."

"Momma said we could have puppies when they came home for Christmas. Why can't we have them?" Isaac frowned at him.

There were times he didn't think the boys really understood what the death of their parents meant. "Remember we have to talk to Vanessa. Show me these fierce kittens."

In the stall, Max sat on the ground with the boys. One of the girls handed him a tiny calico cat, and he laughed as the four kids told him stories about each of the six kittens. Even Tomas managed a few words.

Maybe he could just stay in here. Hiding with the kids might make him a coward, but he was enjoying himself.

Jackie poked her head round the door. "There you are. Hiding?"

Caught. "No." He stood, dusting shavings from his jeans. "They wanted me to see the kittens."

Her dimple went deeper. "If that's what you tell your-self."

"That's my story, and I'm sticking to it."

"They've brought all the food in and we're getting ready to pray." She held her hands out, and her nieces took them.

They turned to the boys. "You can sit with us."

People were gathered in a circle around the table, the men with their hats in their hands. Max ended up next to Jackie, with Tomas on the other side.

Mr. Bergmann stood at the head of the table. He placed his hat on a chair back, and the others followed suit. "Let us join hands and praise God."

Max put his hat on the back of a chair so he could hold Tomas's small hand, and took Jackie's soft one in the other. This basic human contact had been missing from his life.

Tomas pulled on Max's hand.

He leaned down. "What is it?"

The six-year-old got as close as he could. "I don't know how to pray."

"We're just talking to God. No right or wrong way. You don't have to say anything out loud."

With a nod, Tomas closed his eyes.

Max straightened up and found Jackie looking at him.

Mr. Bergmann cleared his throat, and silence fell. His voice filled the room as he prayed. Max was sur-prised by the wave of peace that washed over him. They prayed at the beginning of each rodeo, but here, with these people, it felt more personal. Intimate.

It wasn't just Jackie that hit him hard. It was standing with these strangers. It was odd but a sense of connec-tion settled over him. Maybe it was the presence of his brothers. He sent up his own silent prayer.

Everyone said amen, and Jackie squeezed his hand. He knew it didn't mean anything; it was what you did at the end of a prayer. But it still warmed him.

People moved to the stack of plates at the end of the decorated table, and Max gaped at the amount of food. He counted three types of sweet potatoes, not to mention the smoked, roasted and fried turkeys. He made sure to get behind Tomas and Isaac so he could help them.

Danica's daughters called out to his brothers. "Come on, boys. Let's go down there."

The cowboys had gathered at the opposite end. He'd feel more comfortable with that group. Danica smiled at him. "I'll watch them if you want to go down there."

"Are you sure?" The boys seemed excited about joining the Bergmann family. "Okay."

He looked for Ethan, and spotted him with the group of teens Jackie had introduced him to. He was sitting beside Kelsey and studiously ignoring her.

Max chuckled as he headed for the group of cowboys that sat across from Ethan.

"Hi. Anyone sitting here?"

"Sit. Sit." One of the men waved to a couple of empty chairs.

Max sat and looked down the table. Ethan smiled at him, and they both glanced down the table to Tomas and Isaac. After eating more food than he thought possible, Max sat back and watched his brothers. They all looked happy.

After the pies, Adrian and Reid took the kids out on the four-wheelers to look at some of the animals. Max had doubts about the boys going, but Jackie reassured him that the kids would be safe.

People began to say their goodbyes and leave. Another group followed Mr. Bergmann inside the house to watch a football game. Jackie started putting things in order. Max rested his good shoulder against a stall and watched her scrape and organize dishes. Why was he still in here?

The hairs on the back of Jackie's neck bristled. She looked up to see Max standing there, just watching her.

She wiped her hands on her jeans and pretended she didn't have to straighten all the supplies in the barn. "You can go watch the game with the guys."

"Nah. I'm not much into football." He straightened and walked toward her.

Her breath caught in her throat, and she resisted the urge to back up. "What are you doing, Max?"

"Do you need help?" He scanned the barn. "Your sisters seem to have abandoned you with a huge mess."

"Oh. No, we agreed to clean later. The most important thing is to enjoy our time with family and friends."

"But you're out here, alone. Cleaning."

"Not really. I was just putting a few things back in place." She rubbed her hands against her pants. "Most of my sisters have families here. I don't. They don't need to worry about any of this. And Nikki needs to stay off her feet." Making sure to smile, she tucked a loose strand of hair back into its clip. Why did she feel like she was hiding a dark secret?

Max gathered some drinking glasses and placed them carefully in the bin, lining them up just the way she had. Even her sisters made fun of her for doing that. Max said something she couldn't catch.

She blinked and swallowed the knot in her throat. As a teen, he had been so sensitive and gentle with her. She would get lost in the words he wrote. He had been the only boy she knew who wrote poetry. She could still hear his voice and feel how each word had spoken to her heart. He had talked of the pain and heartache of loss. She had never felt so connected to another person. Max had understood her like no one else; even her twin didn't reach to the buried parts of her heart. But he was a man now. A man with a hard gaze and pride on his shoulders. "I'm sorry. What did you say?"

"I spoke with my uncle." He stopped what he was doing and looked at her.

The depth in his dark eyes pulled her closer. "What… what did he say? Are we good with the buildings?"

He sighed and ran his fingers through his hair. "Sorry. He has some deep, unreasonable hatred for Clear Water."

"Why?" The desertion of hope left her lungs empty. "We didn't do anything to him. Not that I know of, anyway. Your family caused the problems. Your uncle is the worst. He's just left…ugh." She rubbed her temples. "Sorry. I don't understand. How does saving our history hurt him?"

"I don't know why my family has done the things they've done. My father remarried and had me shipped off. I didn't see him for years."

"Years?" She couldn't imagine her father not talking to her, let alone sending her away. Gruff and hard as he could be, she never doubted he loved her. She frowned. "I didn't know that. I thought you grew up in Dallas with your father."

"Nope. When Dad got a new family, the old one had to vanish—or at least get out of his line of vision. Ethan's mom was not a nice woman. Being a stepmother wasn't on her to-do list. Needless to say, motherly instincts and nurturing are not anywhere in her wheelhouse."

"Is that why Ethan's with you?"

"I'm not sure why he wanted to come with us, but I

think that might have something to do with it." He went back to collecting glasses, as though the subject wasn't so heart wrenching. "He hasn't said much, but I don't think he gets along with his stepbrothers in Chicago. We're looking for a family connection. My father never encouraged the whole brother-bonding thing."

With the last glass neatly in line, he placed the silverware into the blue bin. All the pieces faced the same direction.

"Max, I'm glad you brought the boys today. I think they had fun."

The corner of his mouth twitched. "Yeah, and no one threw rocks at us. I can't count how many times someone mentioned the thousand acres of thistles I need to eradicate."

She wrapped her arms around her waist. "Please, don't give up with your uncle. I just know if we're persistent and lay out our reasons, we can bring him around."

With a shake of his head, Max gathered up more utensils. "I don't think so. He's beyond stubborn."

She stopped what she was doing and rested one hand on her hip. "Max?"

He looked up at her. "I can't promise anything, but I was thinking you made a good point. I didn't want anything to do with the family business, but I am a Delgado. It's time I have a say in what happens on the ranch. My dad had fifty-five percent of the business. That means between me and my brothers, we have our father's shares. There might be a way, but I'm not sure I have the time to fight him."

She narrowed her eyes. "What do you want?"

"I'm not going to say yes to something I can't promise."

"You have something I want. What do you want?"

He laughed. "You could watch the boys for a few hours. They barely sleep. I haven't been on a bull in too long." Grinning, he moved away from her. He might be joking, but she wasn't.

Then she recalled his injuries. "Should you be riding a bull? What about your eye? And your shoulder?"

"It's been long enough. I just need to get back on, and the boys make that impossible." He crossed his arms and leaned his hip on the edge of the table. "Don't get me wrong. I'm really glad I'm here with the boys, but it is so much more than I realized. There is no time to do anything if I want to keep them safe."

"Seriously, I'll do it. I'll watch the boys. And you'll let me have access to the old settlement? We could reopen the old road. It's on the edge of the ranch, between our property lines."

"I can't let you do that. I don't even understand why it's on our land. They just abandoned it and started a new one?"

"The story goes that the Delgados initially donated the land and buildings. The ranch was part of an original Spanish land grant when Texas was still part of Mexico. Your family has been here longer than anyone else. Then the Lawsons and a couple of other families settled along the river. They wanted to establish a town here and asked your family to help. It was a real community town raising. The town started growing." Making the last fold in a tablecloth, she turned and looked at him.

"That's when your family wanted to change the name of the town and charge everyone for the buildings and the businesses. They said it was their land and they had all the county records. One of your ancestors was the mayor. Another was the sheriff. Accusations of voting fraud and ties with Mexican gangs got tossed around.

So, in the middle of the night the Bergmanns, Lawsons and a couple of other men went in and stole all the official records. They moved the county seat to a new building, where Clear Water sits now. It took them a few years, but they built a new school and church, along with several other buildings. They added the courthouse and blocked your family from running for any government position. Your family fenced off the buildings and dammed up the river. It got ugly. Shootouts and everything. The Texas Rangers had to come in and settle everyone down. It was a mess."

"This all happened, like, over a hundred years ago, right?"

She grinned. "Yeah. Small towns have the longest memories, but you can help rewrite the way Clear Water remembers the Delgados. You can make it right and restore the original buildings our families raised together."

"You do realize this is crazy?"

"It's what our mothers were working on together." She had to get him to see how important it was to finish what their mothers had started.

Deep creases formed on his forehead. "I thought your mother was fighting with mine. That's how the accident happened. Your mother—"

"Who told you that? I have the letters our mothers wrote to each other. They were working with the city council to make the buildings official historical landmarks and trying to convince your family that this was the right thing to do. Your mother wanted to restore your legacy. It's in her letters. I can show them to you. They're part of the records at the county museum."

Max just stared at her, openmouthed. Then he blinked a couple of times and turned away. "No. As much as I would love for you to watch the boys, I can't let you do that. What if you start all this work, then my uncle comes in and takes it all?"

"If it's going to be ready for Christmas I need to start now. I'm willing to take the risk. Let's make a deal. I'll watch the boys so you can—" she waved her hand at him "—do more damage. And you will work on your uncle."

He shook his head. "I can promise to talk to my uncle, but that's it. I don't—"

The tall barn door slid open, and they both turned. Danica slipped inside, rubbing her arms to warm herself up. "I told Nikki you were in here cleaning. She said you'd gone with the kids, but they're back." She looked at the lined-up bins and organized dishes. "Max. You're an enabler."

His gaze darted to Jackie. "I was just helping."

Danica placed her hands on her hips. "Hence the word *enabler*. She promised to hang out with the family before she went about organizing everything. We agreed to come back and clean all this after we got the first round of Christmas decorations out, but she just can't help herself." Danica shook her head. "Are you going to join us or stay out here and clean? This is my first Christmas to decorate my own house, and Daddy's brought over a bunch of the family ornaments and decorations. The kids are all excited. Please, Jackie?"

"Of course, I'll come and help." She turned to Max. "You and the boys can join us."

Max straightened up from the table he'd been leaning on. "It's a good time for us to head out. Thank you so much for the invite."

As the three of them approached the back porch, his littlest brothers came running down the steps, their faces glowing with excitement. "Max, the animals were awesome. We saw bears! Real bears and deer and donkeys."

The boys spoke so fast on top of each other he couldn't tell who was saying what.

Tomas was smiling bigger than Max had ever seen. "There's a ton of animals here. They save them and turn them back to the wild."

"That's cool. Tell everyone thank you. We're going back to the cabin."

Their faces fell. "No, they invited us to help decorate for Christmas."

"That's a family event."

"But they want us to go, and we've never decorated for Christmas."

Jackie's heart clogged her throat. She glanced at Max. His jaw was set.

Tomas's eyes got even bigger, pools gathering on his bottom lashes. "Suzie and Lizzy said we'd get to hang stars and eat cookies. Please, Max."

She looked at her sister and saw the same sadness she was feeling. Danica knelt beside the boys, but looked up at Max. "It's not just for family. I say the more the merrier. You have to come. We have Christmas music, and with the cold weather we'll even make hot chocolate and read our first Christmas story."

"Please, Max. We'll be good." Both boys had perfected the puppy dog eyes. The bottom lip just completed the look.

Jackie couldn't stand it. "Max. Come on. If you don't want to come, that's fine. The boys will be safe with us, and in a couple of hours we'll bring them to you."

Max stuffed his hands into his pockets. "Are you sure?"

Isaac moved closer to him. "Come with us? It will be fun."

Max looked at Jackie. Doubt clouded his eyes.

Despite the churning in the pit of her stomach, she made sure to smile at him. "Come on. You can do this. Memories are the most precious gifts we have." She bit her lip as she gazed down at the smallest Delgados.

Danica stood. "Don't be a Scrooge, Max."

He nodded as if he was volunteering to go behind enemy lines. The boys cheered and ran to the house.

As they followed, Jackie was having serious doubts about her ability to hang out with Max and not be moved by him and the boys. She had never met anyone who needed family and love more than these brothers. It was very dangerous for her heart.

Did she want more than just the buildings? "Max." She couldn't afford to lose her heart, but the fire in the pit of her stomach was there to save her mother's dream. She waited for him to join her on the porch. "So about the buildings. You didn't say yes."

"Are you half pitbull? I can't say yes. Not until I get something in writing from my uncle."

"I'm a big girl. I understand the risk, and I'm willing to take it. I have faith that God brought us here to this point for a reason. I'm going to trust Him." She had to because she couldn't trust herself.

"You might be more stubborn than all the Delgados put together."

"When I believe in my mission, yes. Our mothers were working together to make this happen. This is our chance to carry on and make their dream become reality. I know this is what I'm meant to do. Please say yes. If it goes wrong, then it's all on me, but in the meantime you can get on the bulls. We can both win here."

Danica stuck her head out the back door. "Are y'all coming in? The kids are waiting."

Max tilted his head back as if he was looking for answers in the night sky. "We'll talk."

On impulse she hugged him, but he stiffened and she backed off. Embarrassed, she turned and rushed into the house. That was stupid. Max was not the teen boy she had fallen in love with. And worse, she was the reason their mothers had not been able to complete their mission.

Chapter Seven

Max wrapped his hands around the hot coffee mug. It gave him something to do while the boys mixed right in with the Bergmann clan as if they'd always been a part of a big family. He, on the other hand, was having a hard time breathing. His shirt was getting tighter around his neck. Ethan had ended up going with the other teens to hang out.

What had he been thinking? He couldn't let her talk him into working on those old buildings. She was going to get hurt, and it would be his fault.

He checked his watch. Another hour and he was picking up Ethan. Mr. Bergmann had given him a few hostile glares, but the rest of the Bergmanns didn't seem to mind having a few Delgados in their home.

Jackie laughed as she tried to untangle a strand of lights, the colors reflecting on her face. His brothers joined the three girls around the tree as they passed the Christmas lights around and back to Jackie. "Now the ornaments. The biggest ones on the bottom."

Tomas ran over to Max. "Look at this one. It's a cowboy like you. I want to put it up high. Can you help me?"

They weren't going to let him sulk in the corner. He

ruffled Tomas's hair. "Sure." He picked him up with his good arm, but it still pulled on the broken collarbone. Careful of his brother's broken arm, he walked to the tree. "Where do you want him?"

Tomas looked at Jackie. "Here?"

"Right next to the angel? Looks like a perfect place for the cowboy."

Tomas's tongue stuck out as he leaned in and carefully hooked the ornament on the branch.

Isaac was helping the girls tie bows around the branches.

"It looks great, guys." Jackie clapped.

All four Bergmann sisters started singing along with the song playing. Their smiles and glances at each other made him even more aware of the family connection he and his brothers were missing.

"I'll Be Home for Christmas" moved him in a way no Christmas song ever had. Tonight, the song gave him a knot in his throat. He'd never had a home to return to. Would this make it worse for the boys when it was time for him to return to the road?

Danica clapped her hands. "Everyone ready for a story?" She picked up a picture book from a stack on the coffee table. "Come on, everyone, you can sit around the tree. Daddy, are you ready?"

Mr. Bergmann stood and handed a book to one of his sons-in-law. "I think Reid should read it this year."

There was a sudden hush in the room, and everyone seemed to hold their breath.

The other man's eyes flashed with surprise. "Really?"

Jackie put her hand to her chest. Max leaned down. "I take it this is a big deal?"

She nodded, and her hand went to his arm. "Daddy always reads the story on the first night. Always." It looked like she might start crying. Max shifted his weight and put a hand on hers. He took a slow sip of his coffee. He needed to keep it casual, even though he felt anything but.

One of her nieces ran over to them and grabbed her aunt's free hand. "Come on, Aunt Jackie, Daddy gets to read the story tonight."

Jackie moved away from him and joined the kids on the floor. Reid sat in a large overstuffed chair, his wife nestled next to him. He was flipping through the pages of a picture book. One of their daughters climbed into her mother's lap. The other one sat in Jackie's crossed legs. Tomas sat down next to them and she smiled and pulled him closer. Isaac was on Jackie's other side, with Mia, Nikki's stepdaughter, next to her father. It was a Christmas scene right out of a Norman Rockwell painting. His holidays were always more along the lines of *The Scream.*

Tomas smiled uncertainly up at Jackie and she kissed the top of his disheveled hair. Max understood the desire to sit next to her. She had a warmth about her that drew him in. It made him feel that everything would be okay if he could just stay near her. If he could make her smile and hear her laugh.

Reid's baritone voice started reciting the first Christmas story, with angels proclaiming the news and wise men seeking the Christ Child.

Max sat his cup down and looked for an exit. He needed fresh air. When he slipped out the back, the cold wind hit him in the face.

He walked to the end of the small porch and leaned one hip on the railing. Would he ever be able to give the boys these kinds of family traditions?

The door eased open. He turned, expecting Jackie.

It wasn't Jackie, but her father. "Max."

He had a feeling he was about to get a lecture.

"Mr. Bergmann." Max studied the moon hanging low over the horizon. No stars out tonight.

Silence hung between them for a while. Then the older man cleared his throat. "Why are you here?"

Why was he here, at the Bergmann home? His brain was a tangled mess, so he decided to misunderstand the question. "My uncle wants to sell the ranch and get it off our books. I thought it would be a good time to get to know my brothers before we go our separate ways."

"Why are you hanging out with my daughter again?"

"She's the one that came charging out to the ranch before the sun had even set on my first day back in town. Your family keeps including my brothers in your holiday stuff. I'd planned to clean up the ranch and leave without seeing anyone in Clear Water."

"Leaving is something your family is good at. You could have said no when you were invited to dinner."

Max looked down at his boots. "You're right. I could have, but I'm glad I didn't. My brothers needed this. So, thank you for giving them something I couldn't."

"Your uncle is really going to sell the place without ever stepping foot in Clear Water again? You'll be gone soon?"

"That's the plan." This whole conversation wasn't sitting well with him. Like he wasn't good enough to breathe the same air as the folks of Clear Water. As Jackie.

"My daughters are very open, loving people. They aren't always smart with their hearts."

"Nikki and Danica seem happy."

He snorted. "After years of heartbreak that I couldn't fix." Mr. Bergmann took a step closer to the railing.

"The Delgados have given nothing to Clear Water." Hard eyes stared at Max. "You have a way of using people, then discarding them."

"I've never used anyone here."

Mr. Bergmann shook his head and looked over the hills. "That's all you've done for generations. Your grandfathers, your father and your uncle. You all leave people behind once you've got what you wanted. I'm the one that stepped in and helped Joaquin when his father abandoned him and his mother."

Okay, that was from out of nowhere. "What does that have to do with my family?" But after hearing bits of conversations and catching telling glances, he was starting to worry he had more family here than his brothers. What had his father done?

"You really don't know?"

"Maybe if you told me what we were talking about I could join the conversation." His stomach churned, rebelling against the coffee.

"Joaquin is your uncle's son. I won't call him a Delgado because he's loyal and hardworking. He stayed and took care of his mother when most people would have walked away. Your uncle walked away, right back to his wife." Disgust dripped from each word.

Max's thoughts reeled. He gripped the banister. That's why the kid looked familiar. Not because of the rodeo, but because he looked like a Delgado. "Does my uncle know?" As messed up as his family was, he couldn't imagine Rigo purposefully denying a son. Even though his father had never been there for him emotionally, he'd always made sure Max had what he needed.

"Everyone knows."

"How old is he?" Max was getting a sick feeling in his gut.

"Twenty-two."

That gave him a headache. Max turned and leaned back on the railing, considering the house. The perfect image of a family gathered around the hearth. "Rigo's daughters are twenty-four and twenty-one." Did his aunt know? What was he going to do with this information?

His phone alarm went off. "I need to go pick up Ethan." Perfect timing for him to get out of this conversation. More wrongs heaped on the Delgado name. Everyone had a reason to hate his family, and he was tired of being on the defensive. As he went in to get the boys, he felt like a coward, but what else could he do? Call his uncle? Tell Joaquin that he was sorry his family had deserted him?

Everyone looked up at him as he walked into the room. "It's time to leave, boys."

Isaac shook his head. "But he's going to read another story."

He didn't blame the boys for wanting to be with the Bergmanns instead of going with him. "No, we've imposed enough."

"What does 'imposed' mean?" Tomas's forehead wrinkled.

"Um…" He'd never had to explain himself before. "Taking advantage of someone's kindness."

Tomas frowned.

Danica laughed. "You are not imposing, Tomas."

"We have to get Ethan."

Jackie stood, holding her nieces' hands. For a moment, she studied him like she was trying to see past his skin. "They could stay. You could join us for breakfast in the morning when you pick them up. We could talk about the buildings."

Mr. Bergmann walked into the room. "The buildings still? I thought you said they weren't giving them up to the city."

"His uncle said no to moving the buildings in to town, but I worked out a deal with Max."

He was about to correct her, but her father's gaze pinned him to the wall. Even though he spoke to Jackie, he stared down Max. "You did, did you? Is that wise?"

"We can work on them right in their original location. It'll save money and time. We can reopen the old entrance that runs between our properties, creating direct access from the highway. It's even better than my first plan."

Her father didn't look like he agreed. "I don't think it's a good idea for you to be out at the ranch alone."

"I wouldn't be alone. Max will be…" Her lips tightened. "Really, Daddy? I'm a grown woman. I can handle myself."

"I just don't want to see another one of my daughters get hurt."

Anger flashed in Jackie's green eyes.

Danica moved to stand next to her sister. "Daddy, maybe we can talk about this later."

Mr. Bergmann glanced at the children. "Come on, Sammi. I'm going home. I'll see y'all tomorrow at the store."

Max waved the boys over to him. "Time to go." He looked at Danica, not wanting to make eye contact with Jackie. "Thank you for including us in today's events. It was fun. Right, boys?"

They both nodded. "Thank you for inviting us." Isaac spoke for his brother.

"Are you going to come Saturday?" one of the girls asked.

Max hesitated. He was sure he didn't want to know. "What's Saturday?"

The other little redhead nodded. "It's even more fun than decorating this tree."

Tomas looked at Isaac, then they both turned to Max. He sighed. "Okay, I'll bite. What is going on Saturday?"

Jackie smiled at the boys. "All the businesses basically have a street party, and we decorate the whole town for our Christmas market days and parade."

"And we can come?" The boys looked as if they were being given the keys to the Magic Kingdom.

She nodded. "Yeah, it's open to everyone." She looked Max square in the eye. "You should join us in the morning."

"Please, Max, please."

Why did they keep inviting the boys? "I don't know. We have to clean the house so that it's livable. There is a lot of dust and critters to move out. We don't have time."

Their faces fell. Why did he have to be the bad guy?

Jackie put a hand on each of their shoulders but looked up at him. "How about I come help you tomorrow, Max? We'll trounce those squatters and reclaim the Delgado rule."

The boys giggled. She brought light to the darkest places. Unfortunately, he had learned that it was safer to avoid the light.

Those green eyes trapped him. He couldn't look away even though he knew he should. Now she was talking directly to him. Listening was probably a good idea.

"—and you can tackle the area with Ethan. After that's all done we can go look at the buildings. The first steps of our deal." She turned back to the boys. "Then on Saturday, I can take you into town, so your brother can do whatever he needs to." She smiled, obviously pleased with herself. "See—a win all the way around."

Tomas twisted and looked up at him. "Can we, Max?"

"I don't need a maid." Now he was sounding grumpy. "We can take care of the house."

Jackie put her hands on her hips. "And fix the arena? And practice on those bulls?"

Danica laughed. "Organizing is her happy zone. You would be doing her a favor."

"Yes!" She glowed with victory. "The house and arena tomorrow, then decorating the town on Saturday."

"No. I can't promise—"

She cut him off. "I know. I know your uncle might swoop in and take the buildings. But if I have any chance of having those buildings ready for Christmas, I already told you that it's a risk I'm willing to take."

"Okay, then. Count us in."

The boys threw their arms around him. This was getting complicated. He had a simple life, and he wanted to keep it that way.

Jackie stood on the porch and watched the truck pull out of her father's driveway. Danica slipped out the door and gently closed the screen. She nudged her sister's shoulder.

"Are you sure you're okay?"

"Why wouldn't I be?" Jackie watched the taillights disappear into the darkness. A coldness gripped her, one that had nothing to do with the wind.

"Oh, I don't know. Maybe the sadness and longing I see in your eyes whenever you look at Max?"

"His life is sad. Longing? Pfft. That's your imagination. Just because you and Nikki are all settled and growing your families doesn't mean I feel left behind."

"That's not what I meant." Wrapping her arm around Jackie's biceps, Danica pulled her closer. "Is that the longing I see? I thought it was the remains of your teenage love. I know how powerful that can be."

"I need to talk to Daddy." Jackie turned toward the door, but Danica kept hold of her arm.

"You know you have my support in whatever you decide to do. If you need to cry, vent or just talk it through, I'm here. Please don't feel like you have to keep it all inside. I've been there and it'll just burn a hole through your heart. Got it?"

"Yeah. Thanks. But really, I'm fine. He'll be gone soon, and I'm closer to getting the buildings than ever before. That's what I want. And more nieces to spoil. A nephew would be nice, too. Seems I've grown fond of being around boys." Before her sister could look too far into her heart, Jackie fled. Straight to her father's house.

He was upset, and she needed to reassure him that she was okay. He had to trust that she was smart enough to do this without getting her heart involved. Maybe if she could convince him, it would become the truth.

Chapter Eight

Jackie beat the morning sun over the hill. She had the best cinnamon rolls next to her and a gritted determination to focus on the goal in front of her—not her teenage cowboy poet who had turned into a good-looking, pessimistic bull rider. The pit of her stomach told her part of his hardness was her fault.

The boys greeted her with so much joy the heaviness on her shoulders lightened. With Ethan herding them, they took the box of baked goods to the kitchen. In the living room piles of curtains, blankets and other sorts of fabric cluttered the floor.

"Looks like you already got started." This she could do.

Max shook his head. "Really, you don't have to do this."

"And when are you going to get everything else done?" She pulled an old book off the shelf and flipped through the pages of Frio Canyon folktales. "Go, and we'll take care of this."

He disappeared into the kitchen. She heard him talking to the boys. Then she heard the back door open and close. This was a great house, but it needed a good scrubbing and a little bit of love.

In five hours, they had made a huge dent in the mess neglect had created. Hourly breaks with the boys had been fun, too. It was easy to take the time and play with them. They craved any attention and laughed with pure abandon.

Jackie closed the lid on the old washer and took the dry sheets to the dining room. The boys were making a tent. "Careful, boys. There might be spiders, scorpions or snakes curled up sleeping in those old sheets."

Eyes wide, the young brothers dropped the sheet they'd been hiding under. They were on the last load of bedding and curtains. She had wiped down the book shelves and mopped all the floors and now they needed to attack the windows. "Come here, you two. Take this newspaper and wipe the glass on the French doors as high as you can."

"The maid uses newspaper at our house, but we aren't allowed to help."

"On a ranch, everyone has to do their share." She put her hands on her hips and squinted her eyes. "You're old enough, right?"

"Yes, ma'am!" They both nodded with enthusiasm. "And we're strong! See my muscles." Isaac flexed his arm.

"Oh, man, you are!"

Tomas started on a glass door. "Why can't we help Max and Ethan? They're doing cowboy work, and we have to do girls' work."

"Whoa there, partner!" Max stood in the archway dividing the formal living room and the family area. "We have to divide and conquer if we're moving in tonight. There are no girl jobs or boy jobs, just work that needs to be done. When you're taller, you can help dig post holes and fix fences."

Ethan flopped on the dark orange sofa. "Believe me, you'd rather be in here." Head back, eyes closed, it looked as if he had gone to sleep. "Do we have anything to drink?"

"I put some bottled water in the refrigerator." Jackie went back to folding linens.

With a yawn, Ethan went into the kitchen area.

Max checked the boys' work. "This looks great and—" he took a deep breath "—it smells fresh. Good job, boys."

"Opening the windows helped." She kept her head down. Sheets of the poems he had written her had been tucked in an old box in the back of a closet. Now she felt awkward. Did she bring them up? He hadn't even looked at her since he walked in.

He went down on his haunches and wadded up a clean sheet of newspaper. "Here, let me help. This is definitely a two-sheet job. Maybe three." They nodded and followed his example.

She wasn't sure why he thought he was like his father. He was great with the boys. She smiled as the brothers beamed with pride at their clean windows.

Ethan tossed Max a bottle of water. "I'm going to get something to eat. Want anything?"

"You just ate."

With a shrug, he disappeared back into the kitchen.

"I'm going to need a loan just to keep him fed." Leaning against the large dining-room table, he tipped his head back and drank the water.

She made herself stop staring. "I saw your guitar case in one of the rooms."

He frowned, but didn't say anything.

"FAST FIVE" READER SURVEY

Your participation entitles you to:
✳ **4 Thank-You Gifts Worth Over $20!**

Complete the survey in minutes.

Get **2 FREE** Books

See inside for details.

Dear Reader,

Since you are a lover of our books, your opinions are important to us... and so is your time.

That's why we made sure your **"FAST FIVE" READER SURVEY** can be completed in just a few minutes. Your answers to the five questions will help us remain at the forefront of women's fiction.

And, as a thank-you for participating, we'd like to send you **4 FREE THANK-YOU GIFTS!**

Enjoy your gifts with our appreciation,

Pam Powers

To get your
4 FREE THANK-YOU GIFTS:

✱ Quickly complete the "Fast Five" Reader Survey
and return the insert.

"FAST FIVE" READER SURVEY

1	Do you sometimes read a book a second or third time?	○ Yes ○ No
2	Do you often choose reading over other forms of entertainment such as television?	○ Yes ○ No
3	When you were a child, did someone regularly read aloud to you?	○ Yes ○ No
4	Do you sometimes take a book with you when you travel outside the home?	○ Yes ○ No
5	In addition to books, do you regularly read newspapers and magazines?	○ Yes ○ No

YES! I have completed the above Reader Survey. Please send me my 4 FREE GIFTS (gifts worth over $20 retail). I understand that I am under no obligation to buy anything, as explained on the back of this card.

❏ I prefer the regular-print edition
105/305 IDL GM35

❏ I prefer the larger-print edition
122/322 IDL GM35

FIRST NAME | LAST NAME

ADDRESS

APT.# | CITY

STATE/PROV. | ZIP/POSTAL CODE

Offer limited to one per household and not applicable to series that subscriber is currently receiving.
Your Privacy—The Reader Service is committed to protecting your privacy. Our Privacy Policy is available online at www.ReaderService.com or upon request from the Reader Service. We make a portion of our mailing list available to reputable third parties that offer products we believe may interest you. If you prefer that we not exchange your name with third parties, or if you wish to clarify or modify your communication preferences, please visit us at www.ReaderService.com/consumerschoice or write to us at Reader Service Preference Service, P.O. Box 9062, Buffalo, NY 14240-9062. Include your complete name and address.

LI-817-FF18

"You spent a lot of time playing it. Maybe you can play for the boys later." Sweet memories made her smile. When she moved her gaze from the boys to Max, the soft feeling vanished. His eyes were cold and his jaw hard.

He crushed the water bottle in his fist and threw it in the trash can. "It's empty." His voice gruff.

"Oh." She hesitated. Picking up the old tin box full of pages of his poems, she held it up for him to see. "But this isn't. Look what I found." Max didn't share her excitement.

Standing, he popped his knuckles. "You can throw them away. They're trash. They should've been burned with all the others." He walked to the kitchen doorway. "Ethan! Get the rest of the newspapers and help Isaac and Tomas finish the doors and windows. They need to be done before we eat lunch." The easygoing Max was gone. The boys looked at her as if asking what had gone wrong in the last few minutes.

Ethan appeared, a half-eaten sandwich in his hand. "But I'm—"

Max cut him off with a glare.

Head down, Ethan joined his younger brothers. "Yes, sir."

Max headed out the front door.

Jackie tucked the box of poems under one arm and followed him. He stood on the edge of the concrete porch, the valley stretching out around them. Max's fingers tapped the sides of his thighs as he scrutinized the surrounding area. The need to escape was written all over him.

"What's going on? I thought you would be happy that we found these. It's like a lost treasure. You were always writing something. If you didn't have paper, you used napkins. Once you wrote right on my arm."

Ignoring her, he walked to the fence that enclosed the tree-covered yard. Bracing his palms on the top rail and one boot on the bottom, he took a deep breath as if he was trying to look relaxed. But the tension in his jaw gave him away.

"I remember you poring over every word and note, Max. You should read some of the fun ones about the rodeo. The boys would love it."

"It's stupid gibberish and a waste of time. They should've been trashed with the others. I didn't know any had survived."

"Things that bring us joy are gifts, not something you toss in a box and forget. I remember your voice as you read each word to me. It was like you knew about all the hurt and fear that I had hidden inside me."

"Stop." He lowered his head.

"Why?" She stood next to him, the tall oaks creating a spotted canopy overhead. Thinking of the kid he was, she could see wisdom beyond his teenage years. "What did you mean, 'they should've been trashed'?"

He rested his chin on his crossed arms. A deer snorted somewhere in the cedar break. The silence between them grew heavy.

He cleared his throat. "I was doing some research on out-of-control thistle."

"Max."

"Burning them is the best option. I finally got some good news, though. This is the best time of year to do it, while they're dormant."

"What happened with your poetry?" She reached out to touch his arm, but he shifted and her hand dropped. She persisted. "We used to spend hours just talking about things. Life."

"My father… Listen, Jackie. You want access to the

old buildings? We'll work out a deal, but our past is off the table. I was a stupid kid on so many levels. I had to…" He waved his hand toward the box. "After your father found us at the dance, he made it clear what he thought of me. You left with him. I had my grandfather take me to Dallas to confront my father. I wasn't going to let him ignore me anymore. I wanted to find out from him what happened, but he wouldn't talk. All he said was that he didn't have time to deal with…" He pressed his lips into a thin line, then tightened his grip on the railing. "It doesn't matter what he said. He told me to go back to my grandfather's. I stole one of his trucks instead and drove here to Clear Water. I thought if I could talk to you, we'd fix everything. I called."

She closed her eyes, remembering their last conversation. "You were here when you called?"

"Yeah. You made it clear that Bergmanns didn't hang out with Delgados." He shrugged. "Needless to say, my father was furious. He came to the ranch to make sure I knew where I stood. That was the last time I tried to… It was over. You were gone, and I was no longer his son." Eyes closed, Max shook his head. "Nothing else to talk about. I had to grow up. I broke my guitar and burned my work. I must have missed some, but it doesn't matter. No more wasting time on nonsense."

"Those were never a waste of time." She had pushed him away. Her father had been so upset, and she had been shocked to learn that the boy she had fallen in love with had lost his mother because of her.

Caught between her father and Max, she hadn't known which way to turn. From the time of the accident, she'd done everything she could to take the sadness out of her father's eyes. But Max had been hurt, too. She couldn't make both men happy.

There was no way she could ever fix the mistake she had made. All she could do for now was stay focused on her mission. "You're right. I think it's past time to see the condition of the buildings. For our mothers."

"You're not going to let this go, are you?"

"I'm too close. Max, I—"

"I'm going to finish the last of the fencing. We can head out to look at the buildings and the old entrance after lunch." He shoved his hands in his back pockets.

She put the lid back on the tin box. "Thank you. What about these?"

He backed away from the fence. "The fireplace is working. They would actually be useful there."

There had to be a way to reach him. "Max—"

He cut her off with the same glare he had shot Ethan.

"What?" She tilted her head and raised one eyebrow. "I was just going to suggest using them to start a fire to roast hot dogs for lunch."

With a slight pull to the corner of his lips, he shook his head.

Her heart ached. "Can I have them?"

"Whatever." He shrugged. "I have work to do. Send Ethan out." He lifted his hat to push his hair back. With the black Stetson back in place, he walked away without looking back.

As a teen, he had been so idealistic. She had loved that about him. He had been so romantic and sensitive. And he'd ridden a horse like he'd been born on one.

How had he become so cold and hard? She looked down at the poems. He had shared all his dreams and fears with her back then. His writing had been full of questions about life, about the world, about her. The desire to please his father. Some expressed deep sadness over the death of his mother. A loss they had both connected over.

She wanted to cry for everything they had lost because of one careless action on her part.

Wiping her face with the back of her hand, she made sure the boys wouldn't see any tears. She was not throwing the poems away.

Max pulled his truck into the backcountry road that ran along the east of the ranch. All through lunch, he had managed to avoid any talk about his poems and songs. It brought back the memories he'd worked hard to bury. The night he had found out who Jackie was, she had walked away from him. He had tried to blame her father, but she had made it clear that her father's opinion was hers, too.

At that point he had wished his heart was made of stone. She didn't want him to bother her anymore. He'd been a fool all the way around.

His jaw was starting to hurt. He needed to get out of his head.

"I want to work in a feed store when I grow up." Isaac didn't like silence. "Then I can have as many dogs, cats and horses as I want."

Ethan rolled his eyes. "Yesterday you wanted to be a bull rider and a race car driver."

Isaac crossed his arms. "I can be all of those if I want to. Right, Max?"

Jackie laughed. "You would have to work very hard to get all that done. What about you, Ethan? What are your plans for the future?"

He shrugged. "I don't know. Go to Yale or Columbia and major in law."

Max eyed the teen in the rearview mirror. "You don't

look very excited about that. Our father wanted me to get into a top business school. Your stepfather and mother are both lawyers, aren't they?"

"What I really want to do doesn't make any money. It is about as stupid as being a race car driver or…" He jerked his head down.

"Or a bull rider?" Max chuckled. "Our father didn't support my plans until I was ranked and started making money. Sometimes being a little stubborn pays off."

Jackie chuckled. "A little?"

He grinned, but went on like she hadn't questioned him. "Or maybe the drive to prove the old man wrong pushed me. The point is that people said I was crazy, but I made it work. What is it you really want to do?"

Ethan crossed his arms and shrugged. His gaze stayed focused on the surrounding hills. "Music." His voice was so low it was hard to hear him.

"Really?" She nudged Max on the shoulder and sent him a huge grin.

He shook his head. He knew precisely what Ethan faced from his family, and it wasn't warm wishes and support. Music would not be on the list of approved career choices for either family. "You want to make a career out of music?"

"I know it's stupid, but I'm good at dropping mixes. I like making new beats and sounds. But Mom said it was a waste of my time."

Jackie pushed his arm again. He glanced at her, one eyebrow raised. What did she want from him? "Life can be tough when you want to do something outside of the family norm."

Another pop on his arm told him she wasn't happy with his advice. He lifted his shoulders. "What?" he mouthed.

Her lips went flat, and she shook her head at him. She turned back to Ethan with a smile, then rested her arm on the back of Max's seat. Her hand brushed his shoulder, and his breath caught at the casual touch. He swallowed and gripped the steering wheel, focusing on the road ahead.

She went on as if touching him was no big deal.

It's not a big deal. It shouldn't be, anyway.

"Ethan, nothing is wrong with that if it's what you want to do. When you want something that is seemingly out of reach, you'll just have to work twice as hard to get it. It doesn't always come easy, but that can be a good thing. The harder we have to work for something, the sweeter the accomplishment feels."

She looked back at him. Her family supported each other. She didn't get it. When he didn't jump into the conversation, she went on without him.

"I basically work in the construction industry. I'm sure Max had to work odd jobs before he started making money riding bulls."

"Yep." He nodded.

"The thing is, when you love something, you have to find ways to make it work. I love the lumberyard and working with the historical society to restore old buildings. If you love what you're doing, life is so much better."

"I want to do something—anything—with music. I can't imagine doing anything else. Did you always want to ride bulls?"

Isaac turned to Ethan. "He used to write poems. Jackie found a box full of them."

Ethan leaned forward as far as his seat belt would let him. "Really? Like sonnets and haiku? Man, that sounds lame." He had a ridiculous grin on his face. "I can just imagine what Dad thought about that. But you ended up doing something cool. The last summer I spent with Dad, I saw all the rodeo pictures of you in the offices and the stores. The ones of me were gone."

"Ethan, there were no pictures of me until I started ranking in the top twenty." Why did their father treat his sons as if they were disposable?

The kid looked so dejected. Jackie gave him another say-something look.

God, I want to be different from my father. Give me the words.

He knew this was an opportunity to build a better relationship with his brother. "Ethan." He waited for eye contact. "A couple of times when I spoke with him, he said you were at the offices. He would brag about you and told me how you loved the family business, even as a little guy. You were about the age of double trouble here." He winked at the little ones.

Of course, his father was using it to make sure Max knew what a failure he was. No reason for Ethan to know how much he had resented his little brother at the time.

"I got to spend summers with him until about five years ago." The pain in Ethan's eyes was substantial as he glanced at his five- and six-year-old brothers.

Max briefly closed his eyes. His father had been a jerk, but saying that now wouldn't help any of them. "He loved the business more than anything else. It consumed him. Which is why, starting right now, we are making a vow to always be here for each other, no matter what."

Jackie squeezed his shoulder. He glanced at her, and her look of pride and love walloped him upside his head. For a second, it felt as if she could see to the bottom of his heart. Then she broke eye contact and turned to the boys. "Family is about supporting and loving each other, even when we mess up."

Swallowing the knot back down, Max continued. He needed to make them understand they were family, even when they weren't together. "Ethan, whatever you decide to do, I'll be there. None of us are successful right away, but if you want something, you have to be willing to fight for it. To work through the failures, and get up after you're knocked down. My faith in God has gotten me through some dark times. He is the Father we can completely trust. I promise if you call me, I'll help you brush the dirt off."

Isaac clapped. "Jackie said that Max wrote a poem about eating dirt."

Jackie smiled. "He wrote some funny ones and some beautiful poems. Sometimes he would put them to music. I would sit for hours and listen to him."

Ethan sat back in his seat, still smiling like a loon. "Wow. The secret life of bull rider Maximiliano Delgado. Maybe I can put your poems to music and make a bunch of money. Then my mom couldn't say anything." He looked out the window, but he was grinning this time.

Suddenly his head whipped around. "Wait. You wrote her poems? You did used to date!"

Max shook his head at Ethan. "We're not going to talk about this."

"It was a long time ago." Apparently, Jackie had no problem sharing their past. "One summer we met on the rodeo circuit. I ran barrels and poles. I thought he was the cutest cowboy with a really sweet heart. And, man, could he ride and rope. He was doing all-around back then. It was before his PBR fame. He was with his grandfather and uncles. I didn't even know he was a Delgado from Clear Water."

Ethan leaned forward, his arms on the back of the seat in front of him.

"What happened when you found out who he was? Did you dump him because he was a Delgado?"

She pulled away. "It was complicated. I remember him playing the guitar. You two have music in common." Sadness clouded her smile.

Why was she sad? He'd been the one left behind. He'd even run away to see her, but she still wouldn't talk to him. The poems and songs had been a waste of time and energy.

His knuckles hurt from the grip he had on the wheel. He didn't want to think about the senseless thoughts he'd written down, or how his father had reacted to his writings. Jackie had that poor-sad-baby look in her eyes. He didn't need her pity.

The mood in the truck turned heavy and everyone retreated to their own corner.

Max glanced at his brothers. He wanted the smiles back. "So, who wants to have a huge ranch-sized bonfire?"

All eyes turned to him. He glanced at Jackie. "Who do I talk to about doing a controlled burn to get the thistle cleared? I thought we could do one pasture at a time, but I'm not sure. The last thing we need to do is burn down the whole county."

"The extension agent, Robert Cornelis, would be a good place to start." She seemed eager to change the subject, too.

Ethan cleared his throat. "So, why don't you play your guitar anymore?"

Max growled. The teen clearly did not get the memo.

He didn't want to think about that life. No point dragging all this stuff out.

Ethan sat back. "For Christmas every year, I asked for a guitar. I got professional golf clubs. I hate golf. Mom made me join the Japanese language club and the honor society. They look better on a résumé."

"Résumé?" Jackie looked at Max as if he had something to do with it. "You're a freshman in high school."

"Never too early—" Max stopped emulating his father midsentence when he realized Ethan was saying the exact same thing.

"—to build your future," Ethan finished, a slight tug at the corner of his mouth. "I guess you heard it, too. There's no future in music."

"We want a guitar!" Isaac yelled, oblivious to the seriousness of the discussion. "And drums. Momma said we could have puppies, but no drums."

"Momma said we'd get the puppies once she came home," Tomas said in a quiet voice as if he was afraid to upset someone.

"But she's not coming home, is she?" Isaac asked. The heavy sadness filled the cab.

Lost in thought, trying to find the right words, Max almost missed the turn. The road was scarcely there. Shrubs and vines covered the fence and gate. He hit the brake a little too hard.

"Sorry about that. Boys, your mom is always going to be with you in your heart." He really wanted to talk about something else. *God, please give me something.*

Jackie touched the hand he had on the gear shift. "I lost my mother at about your age. So did Max. But we have memories and pictures. Your brother's right—she will always be in your heart. You have pictures and can talk to each other about your memories."

Acid burned his gut. He didn't have memories of his mother, not a single picture. Maybe he needed to fight his uncle a little harder for these buildings. Putting the truck in Park, he stared at what used to be an entrance. This didn't look promising. "I'm not sure we'll be able to get in this way."

"I brought gloves and clippers. If you don't have some basic tools, you can use mine."

"I'm fine. I also have tools." He wasn't sure why he felt he had to defend himself.

She grinned as she stepped down from his truck.

"Can we help? I want to use tools!" Isaac undid his seat belt.

"I think it might be safer for you in the truck." Max eyed the roadside jungle.

"Let us help." Tomas was scrambling to get out.

"Stay close to the truck and away from the road. Ethan, will you keep them close?"

"Yeah. As long as they don't run away."

"We didn't run away! You ignored us."

"Boys." He glanced at Jackie. She was already pulling tangled vines away from the old gate.

She looked over her shoulder. "You might want to keep them in the truck. Their tennis shoes don't offer any protection from rattlesnakes."

"Snakes?" Ethan froze, his eyes darting over the area. His body didn't move a muscle.

Isaac jumped from the truck. "I want to see a snake."

Ethan grabbed him by the shoulder. "She said 'rattlesnake.' The kind that kills you. Get back in the truck."

"I don't want to." Isaac tried to pull his shoulder out of Ethan's grip, but the teen was not letting go.

Jackie stopped and looked back at them, hands on hips. "Why don't you get in the bed of the truck? You'll be safe in there, and you can warn us if you see anything."

Ethan picked Isaac up. He swung him through the air and plopped him in the back of the truck. "Come on, Tomas."

Jackie went back to pulling weeds from the desolate road. Digging through his toolbox, Max found another pair of gloves.

Before taking a step, he looked at the ground. He really hated snakes. With a deep breath, he joined her. *Please, don't let there be snakes.*

No-trespassing signs were posted all over the high fence.

Max chopped away thick grapevines until he found the chain. "We're going to have to cut off the lock." Looking past the fence, he searched for the old route. "I'm not sure this even counts as a road anymore. You know, those buildings might be gone by now."

Jackie straightened and wiped her forehead with the back of her hand. "I have not fought this hard or come this far to give up now. You told Ethan that sometimes you fall, but you have to get back up." She threw another thick grapevine onto the pile she had started. With more force than she probably needed, she attacked the rest of the vine. "Since you're the owner, I'll let you cut the chain. I don't want to get charged with trespassing."

He watched her for a bit longer, then cut the chain. It didn't give easily. When it dropped to the ground, he wasn't sure why he felt like he was the one trespassing.

Then again, he'd never felt he belonged anywhere. Except for that one summer.

She should have driven her own car. With each bump, she had to brace herself from colliding into Max. Being this close set her nerves on edge. Her heart was breaking for him and his brothers. They needed someone to love them unconditionally.

But this adventure was not about Max. It was what her mother had wanted, and it would make her dad happy.

The first building came into view, and her heart sank.

The roof was gone, and all the windows were broken. The porch had collapsed. Light streamed through the boards that made up the walls. Not much of the building was left, and the one on the opposite side of the road was even worse.

She would not cry, she told herself. These were just the outbuildings. Probably nothing more than shacks when they were new. According to some letters and a couple of photos, the church and school had been built with limestone.

"Those buildings look like good candidates for my uncle's project," said Max.

The road had vanished. Slowly Max maneuvered the truck along the side of the property line between the Bergmann and Delgado ranches until he found another path.

Her heart beat a little faster. This was where her mother's family's ranch and the Delgados' met. For generations, there had been disputes over the water and pastures.

The weeds had taken ownership of the old dirt road, and the trees invaded the path. Max had to slow down to make sure they didn't drive over the edge of the cliff.

They turned a sharp curve, and her throat went dry. Her blood stopped flowing. *This is it.*

Nature had erased all evidence of the horrific accident that had changed their families' lives forever. They had driven right over the edge of the bridge. The bridge was no longer there.

Her father had had it demolished. "This is it." Hand pressed against the cool glass, her voice cracked. "The place our mothers died."

Max stopped the truck. "Are you sure?"

Without a thought, she got out of the truck.

The engine cut off. The world slipped away as she saw it the way it was that day. Another cold front had rolled in, pushing the warmer weather out. Pulling her jacket tighter around her didn't do anything against the cold.

"Jackie?"

Max's voice caused her to jump. Glancing over her shoulder, she looked for the boys.

"They're okay. Ethan is singing songs with them." His arm dropped on her shoulders and pulled her close. "Have you come here often?"

Numb, she managed to shake her head. Words got stuck in her raw throat. Wiping her nose, she sniffed. "Not since that day."

"What? You were with them?" He pressed the corner of his forehead against her temple. The black cowboy hat was pushed back.

"No. I was with Daddy when he found them." Time slipped away as the memories bombarded her brain. She blinked fast and hard. "Momma was late. Daddy went looking for her. I had stayed home from school, so he took me with him." She pointed to the other side of the river, where exposed rebar left a scar on the edge of the slope. "They were on our ranch. I don't know if they had just left here or were heading this way. We didn't see the car at first. The second time around, Daddy saw something that caught his eye. He told me to stay in the truck."

She shook her head. "But of course, I didn't. I wasn't very good at listening back then."

Like an old black-and-white film, the scene played in her head. She slipped completely into the past.

The inhuman scream from her father ripped through the air before she was out of the truck. "He yelled my mother's name. It was the most horrific sound I've ever heard." She heard it in her dreams. Even as her mother's voice faded from her memories, she could still hear her father's terror. "I started running. There at the edge, I saw the car."

All she really remembered was shattered glass and blood. There was blood in the water. Things that had been in her mother's car were scattered over the rocks and roots. Her father had thrown something out of the car as he tried to get his wife out.

It was her toy horse, Silver. The white plastic was covered in red. Her heart slammed against her ribs. That was the moment she knew the wreck had been her fault.

Chapter Nine

They stood in silence as time slid into an abyss. He pulled her closer until both of his arms circled her. The brim of his hat cast a shadow over them. The steady rhythm of his heart slowed her rapid beats. Boom, boom. Boom, boom. They fell in step.

"You were here? You saw the crash site?"

A single nod was all she had in her.

His lips were so close to her ear, she heard the slight kick of his breath. "Does your father know you followed him?"

"No."

"Oh, Jackie."

Pulling away, she filled her lungs, then held her breath. "Let's go. I need to go."

Taking her hand, he led her back to the truck and opened the door for her.

He climbed in, turned the key and shifted the gears. But he paused. "Are you sure you want to go on?"

"I've waited so long for this." Then a horrible thought caused her pulse to push hard through her veins. "What if there isn't enough left to save?"

Max reached for her hand. She didn't deserve to be calmed by him. "Then we'll figure something else out."

All three of Max's brothers nodded. Ethan reached over the seat and squeezed her shoulder. "Even if the buildings can't be used, you'll find history."

"You're right." She had to focus on what she could change. "Thank you, guys." She glanced at Max. He looked shaken. She hadn't even thought of him. He hadn't known where his mother had died. "I'm so sorry, Max."

"Not your fault."

But it was. And she was too much of a selfish coward to tell anyone. She bowed her head and prayed for peace and understanding. Turning everything over to God was hard for her, but it was the only way she could survive.

"Look!" Isaac pointed to a rock building with a steeple. "There it is!"

Jerking her head up, she saw it. Her heart swelled. The church was still there. Another building stood across from it. The school was still standing, too. Laughter bubbled up. "There it is."

It didn't take them long to get out of the truck and walk around the building. She followed close behind Max.

The boys skipped and ran around. One of them shouted, "We want to go in."

All the windows and doors had been covered with heavy boards. She turned to Max. "Can we pull those off?"

"No telling what kind of critters have moved in over the years." He didn't have the same enthusiasm as his brothers.

"It looks strong." She laid her palm against the rough stone. "The records state that your family had pieces of stained glass shipped from Italy and commissioned an artist from Mexico to put them back together." She couldn't even imagine what it looked like. Even the best pictures were still grainy. Adrenaline surged through her body. "Max, please. We need to get inside and see how much of it is still intact." She went to his truck and lifted the crowbar from the back.

He reached for the iron, but she stepped away from him. "I saw you flinching when you cut the chain. Your shoulder is still tender."

He growled.

With a grin she couldn't help, Jackie moved past him to the door. "Growl all you want, Delgado. I'm used to working with men at the lumberyard." She wedged the flat end under a board and pushed until it popped loose.

Ethan held Isaac and Tomas by the hands. "Do you need help?" he asked.

Max stuffed his hands in his pockets and rocked on his heels. "Apparently not."

"I don't doubt your manliness." She put her weight into the next board and addressed Ethan. "He already stressed his injury at the gate. I'd forgotten about his shoulder. But I could use a little more muscle."

Isaac jumped up and down. "I want to help. I'm not hurt like Max and Tomas. What can I do?"

As a team, they made quick work of the boards that covered the double doors. But before they could open them, Max called out from the side, "Let's uncover a few windows, too. We'll need as much light as we can get."

When the first window was exposed, she stood back. "Max. These are stained glass, too."

Excitement had her wanting to dance and jump. "It's gorgeous." Blues and greens framed the design, with warm colors in the center radiating from a dove. She touched it, the beauty of the craftsmanship taking her breath. "Let's open the rest."

Carefully they pried the protective boards off the windows. Now they stood where they had started. Her heart pounded. She looked at Max and the boys. They looked back at her.

Max moved to the door. "Are you ready?"

"For some crazy reason, I want to cry." She stood on the threshold of five years of work. "This is what our mothers were fighting to save." With one hand on the door, she paused and looked at Max. "I'm glad we're doing this together. I think they'd like that. They both thought the family grudges were ridiculous."

A slight curl brought the corner of his mouth up. "Then let's do this."

She ran her fingers over the cast-iron door handle. "It's a thumb latch. Look. It has a coat of arms." She looked at Max. "A deer and eagle."

"I've seen that before, at the house." Max looked at the details.

"It's at the offices, too." Ethan peered over her shoulder. "It's the Delgado crest. Uncle Rigo said we came from Spanish nobility."

Max snorted. "He would like to think so."

"With the land grants and coat of arms you might be."

Ethan grinned. "I'm a prince?"

"If you want to be." She pushed the door, but it didn't budge.

Max moved beside her. "Let me."

She narrowed her eyes.

"I promise to use my good shoulder." He was so close his breath brushed her neck.

Needing to put distance between them, she moved out

of the way. With one shove, he had the door open. He stepped aside and held out his arm, inviting her to enter.

Taking a deep breath, she crossed the threshold. Dust, cobwebs and stale air filled the space. A few of the blue floor tiles were cracked, but the damage looked minor. Beyond the altar was a large chamber. She tried the small door. "People were shorter then, I guess. It's stuck."

Max opened it without a problem. He ducked and walked through. "Oh, Jackie. I think you're going to like this."

Stepping in behind him, she took a deep breath. The air seemed fresher in here. Then she looked up. Her breath stopped.

The long, wide room was filled with pews, more than she had expected. They were carved from dark wood, with ornate arms and feet, and lined up like soldiers. She turned to look at the front of the church. The elaborate stained glass was dusty, but color managed to push past and dance along the sunlight.

They stood in silence, all staring at the six-foot design. The top of the window was shadowed, still covered by boards. A cross stood tall in the center, ribbons of flowing water surrounding it. A lamb was at the base.

She gazed up at the beams exposed in the high ceiling, then down the aisle to where Max stood. "Can you imagine the people that came through the doors? The weddings, baby dedications and other life celebrations, along with funerals." She pushed Tomas's thick wavy hair off his forehead. "The church was the hub of the community. I can't wait to see it come alive again with Christmas." She looked at Max. "I'm calling Adrian and the other volunteers. It's in much better shape than

I had even hoped. I think we can have this place ready for the Christmas Eve pageant."

"I don't want to be the bad guy here, but we don't know for sure if my uncle will allow you to do this." He shifted on his feet. "We'll have to wait and see."

The boys had explored every corner of the church and were now bored. Ethan offered to take them outside. With a nod Max agreed. "Stay away from the other buildings until I'm with you."

"Yes, sir." Once they were gone, the church seemed empty without the boys' energy.

Max moved past her and watched the boys go out the door. "I don't know what to do. The plan was to spend some time with them, then we all go our separate ways. Now? I don't know."

He looked so lost.

"Why can't you keep them?" She placed her hand on his arm. He covered it with his and moved it to his chest. The steady rhythm of his heart comforted her.

"I'm not father material. Bull riding is not a life for kids."

"I think you're underestimating yourself. You told Ethan that no one finds success the first time they try something new. This would be the same."

"This isn't about a few bruises. They're kids. Tomas and Isaac are little humans. Ethan is at a pivotal point in his life. Their future and emotional stability are at stake. Tomas broke his arm on my watch."

"Look where we're standing. Everyone told me to give up." She squeezed his hand. "God brought you to the ranch with the boys. Maybe this is where you are supposed to be. You can bring the Delgados back to the Delgado land." Emotions tightened her chest and throat. Her eyes burned. She bit down on her lip. She wasn't going to cry.

He wouldn't understand. She didn't understand. Tears spilled from her lids.

"Jackie? Are you crying?"

She shook her head in denial, but it didn't stop the tears.

He took her in his arms, surrounding her with his warmth and scent of outdoors. For some reason, that made her cry even harder. She was losing her mind and she didn't know how to get it back.

One hand cradled her head against his chest while the other rested on the center of her back. He was muttering Spanish words in her ear, and she couldn't make sense of them. She wasn't sure how long she cried, but it was too long.

Swallowing back the last sobs, she lifted her head but kept her eyes down. There was no way she was making eye contact after that embarrassing outburst. "I'm sorry."

His fingers caressed the back of her neck. "No apologies needed." He pressed his lips against the side of her head. "It's been a rough day. When we finally stop and look around, that's when it hits us. What we've lost." He shrugged. "What we've gained. Cry all you want. When we were Ethan's age, you were always one of the strongest people I knew. I think you're even stronger now."

She pulled back and looked up at him. His gaze moved to her lips, then back to her eyes. He was going to kiss her. His lips touched hers, gentle and soft. Just a whisper of a spring breeze.

"Are we leaving anytime—oh, sorry." Ethan stood at the open door. "Um. I'll be out here." He vanished.

A few steps put much-needed space between her and Max. Being that close was dangerous.

"Jackie." He moved toward her.

She shook her head. "I'm sorry. Thank you for letting me pull it together." Her gaze darted around the room. "Could you pretend this didn't happen?" She waved her hand in a circle. "Whatever happened, or was about to happen, can't happen." *Great, now I'm babbling.*

"Got it. You're a Bergmann, and I'm a Delgado. Sorry, I forgot."

"Max, that's not it. I'm…"

He stared at her.

She was what? *The reason our mothers are dead.*

"It's okay." He ran his hand through his hair and picked up his hat from the front pew. "I'm leaving, anyway."

"Are you sure about that? If you want to keep your family together, there has to be a way. It might not be easy but, Max, family is worth fighting for."

He stopped at the door and looked back at her. "But I'm not sure I'm worth the fight." He slammed his hat on and disappeared through the door.

What had she been thinking? She scanned the church once more. She was standing in the middle of her dream. So why did it feel like she had lost something even more precious?

Chapter Ten

It was Saturday, and the boys had been so excited about coming into town they were up before the sun. He had put them off until after lunch, but finally gave in to their pleas. Even Ethan had mumbled about wanting to go into town. Max slowed the truck to a crawl as they passed the café and feed store.

In the back seat, the boys strained against their seat belts, trying to see everything at once. People were everywhere. There were more pedestrians on the street than vehicles. All the town's four hundred inhabitants, and then some, had to be on the main strip.

All the boys wore wide-eyed expressions of wonder, even Ethan. "Wow. They have Christmas trees all over the place."

Bergmann's Lumber was right in the middle of it all. The two-story limestone building had a deep balcony on the second floor. The building had stood there for over a hundred years and looked like it would last another hundred.

Jackie had every right to be proud of her family. And he was an idiot for trying to kiss her. What had he been thinking?

She had made it clear his attentions were not welcome. He would have thought he had learned his lesson long ago, but apparently, he was a slow learner.

Sammi waved them down from the sidewalk. Max eased the truck to the curb and glanced around, looking for Jackie.

Ethan sat up. "There's Kelsey." He had the door open before Max had the engine turned off. Then he pulled back and sat there, staring at the group of teens.

"What's wrong?"

"Her mom doesn't like me."

"It's just a town Christmas event. There are lots of people here, including Kelsey's brother, right?"

Ethan nodded, but his frown stayed tight.

"Ethan has a girlfriend." Isaac and Tomas giggled from the back seat.

"Shut up." The teen crossed his arms.

"Hey, it's not like you're asking her on a date or anything. You have a right to talk to anyone you want."

"Are you going to ask Jackie on a date?"

"We're not talking about me." That was a whole other issue. "Just go over there and talk to her, or talk to her brother. Sitting here in the truck isn't going to help."

Ethan climbed out of the truck and stood there.

Sammi walked over. "Hey, guys, we were just wondering if you were going to make it into town. Ethan, you should join them. They're decorating one of the trees for silent auction next weekend."

Nodding like he had a clue what she was talking about, Ethan stuffed his hands in his pockets and moved in their direction.

"Make sure you stay where I can see you!" Max hollered, for good measure.

Sammi leaned into the cab with a huge smile. "Don't

worry. They're good kids, and everyone is right here on Main." She looked over into the back seat. "Hey, boys. Y'all ready to get your Christmas on?"

"Yes!" they yelled with excitement. She helped them out of the back seat and winked at Max.

This had been the right thing to do. His brothers needed normal, even if he had no idea what that should look like. People laughed as they hung wreaths, fake snow frosted the windows and Christmas songs floated through the air on unseen speakers.

A cherry picker was parked under a street lamp, hanging green and red banners. He imagined this was about as close as anyone could get to the American dream. All they were missing was real snow to make it a perfect Christmas card.

Stepping onto the sidewalk, Tomas took his hand. He bounced with excitement. "Are we going to get a tree for the house?"

They didn't seem to get the idea that they might not be here for Christmas.

If Vanessa came early enough, he wouldn't have to deal with it. "I'm not sure we have the time."

"There's always time to spread Christmas joy." Jackie had sneaked up behind them, an industrial-sized wheel of lights over her arm.

Sammi appeared between the boys. "I'm going to the courthouse with the ornaments made by the Sunday-school classes." She looked down at them. "My nieces are over there with their mom. You want to come help?" She glanced at Max. "Is that okay?"

"Please, please!" cried the two boys.

"Are you sure? Do you need my help?" answered Max.

"I wouldn't have invited them if I didn't mean it."

She grinned. "We have plenty of help at the square, but Jackie could use you."

There was a sparkle in her eye that had him suspicious.

She pointed to the upper level of their store. "I usually help her with the balcony, but Danica claimed me this year." Her attention went back to the boys. "Come on, let's go in and get the bags."

Placing his hands on their shoulders, Max looked each of the boys in the eye. "You have to stay with Sammi and Danica."

"The one that looks just like Jackie?"

"Yes. No wandering off, no matter what you see. Do you understand?"

In unison, the boys nodded. "Yes, sir!"

They didn't hesitate for a second. They followed Sammi into the building without a backward glance.

It didn't feel right sending them off with someone else.

"They'll have fun," Jackie reassured him, patting his arm. Her hand rested on his sleeve. "My sisters will keep them safe."

He smiled, not sure if he liked the idea she knew what he was thinking. "I should just go to the ranch and get some work done."

"You mean go *hide* at the ranch." Her hand was warm through his heavy jacket. Then she pulled it away, as if she remembered who she was touching. "Come on. It appears I've been abandoned by my whole family. I need to hang the lights and garland on the top balcony. Plus, everyone can have a better look at us up there."

She waved to a group of women who had been staring at them. With a flip of her red braid, she marched past the display windows.

"You mean I'll make an easier target for gossip?"

She rolled her eyes. "You'll be able to see the boys, too."

The bell chimed as he followed her into the store. Inside, the smells of lemon oil and old hardware created a welcoming atmosphere. The small group of men that turned and frowned at him? Not so much.

"Hey, Daddy." Jackie kissed her father's cheek. "Max has volunteered to help me hang the lights upstairs." She flashed him a smile.

The men looked at him. He'd faced two-thousand-pound bulls with more welcoming expressions. He smiled and nodded.

A tall cowboy with a genuine smile held out his hand. "I'm Lawson. Sorry to hear of your loss, but glad you're back. We were just wondering now what your plan is to get the pastures under control. Anything we can do to help?"

Max swallowed his glare and met the man eye to eye. "I've looked into it, but I'm a rodeo guy. Never worked the land. I'm more than willing to hear ideas and pass them on to my uncle. It looks like burning this time of year might be the most effective method. I've put a call in to my uncle to see what he thinks."

The man who spoke to him at the café, Dub Childress, cleared his throat. "Not to start an argument, but we don't much trust your uncle."

"He's in charge."

"Don't you have your father's vote now?" The man's sharp eyes glared at him. "You're not selling to some developer? Some of the best ranches have been lost that way."

He turned from Dub only to find Jackie's dad glaring at him.

Mr. Bergmann stared him down. "But you're letting Jackie work on the old settlement. Is she going to lose that?"

"Daddy, we've talked about that. It's a risk I'm willing to take. These lights are getting heavy, and I need to get them up." Jackie shifted the lights from her left arm to her right.

Max hated that he agreed with her father, but he didn't want to oppose her in front of these men. Putting one hand on her back, he took the lights from her with the other. "Upstairs?"

"Yes." She smiled, and he was momentarily reminded of the girl he'd been obsessed with.

"He's going upstairs with you?" Her father was frowning at him.

"Daddy, could you get the nativity scene down, so we can put it in the window?" Apparently, she was going to ignore her father's last comment.

With a nod to the men, he followed her, their boots clicking on the old wood floor. They passed through an office area and ascended a flight of narrow stairs, their edges worn by years of traffic. "I know you're going to hate this, but I agree with your father. Until I get something in writing you shouldn't do anything to the buildings."

Jackie made straight for the eight-foot glass doors, ignoring him on the subject just like she did her father. They stepped out onto the vast balcony that ran the length of the building. It had to be twelve feet deep. The railing and trim reminded him of an old Western movie.

He gave a low whistle. "I can see a rifleman standing guard up here as trouble rides into town."

She laughed. "You always had such a great imagination. Of course, it is possible. This building has been here since 1886, and I'm sure it's seen plenty of trouble. There are stories about the Bergmanns and Delgados having a showdown right here in front of the store. It wouldn't surprise me if they stationed a few men with guns up here."

He glanced down the main street. From here he could see the courthouse. At the other end of town was a line of shops and a few houses. Smalltown, America, at its quaintest. "It appears be the best view in town."

She started unrolling the string of lights. "Yeah, not much has changed in Clear Water over the years. The new school building has a third floor."

"New?"

She nodded. "It was built in 1937. But it caught fire in '72, so they had to rebuild it."

He shook his head. "That's new?"

"Hey, your family's ranch has the oldest history in town. Don't go throwing rocks."

"No wonder my father and uncle left here. They both love new and modern." *His father.* How did he keep forgetting he was gone? "My father hated anything old. He was always looking for the newest and most improved. Including family."

She stood and reached out to him. "Max, I'm so sorry. Even if you didn't have a good relationship with him, it still hurts to lose him. Maybe more so because you didn't have a chance to mend it."

His heart twisted, but he shrugged it off. "Is there a ladder around here?"

"Ignoring it won't make the feeling go away."

"He's gone, so there's no point. Where's the ladder?"

"Max." She touched his sleeve.

"Ladder?" He had to look away from the concern that was heavy in her gaze. It hadn't helped to talk to his father when he was alive, so there was no point talking about him now.

"Go to the room in the back. There's a closet on the left. It should be there."

He rejoined her a few minutes later, and took a deep breath. "I never thought of Christmas having a smell." Sugar cookies, gingerbread, coffee and crisp air filled with the scent of fresh-cut trees made it feel more like Christmas than anything he'd ever experienced.

"The bakery has delivered the gingerbread pieces for making the houses. And the giant tree for the center of town has arrived." She looked up from her neatly laid-out lights. "It smells delightful, doesn't it?" She rubbed her hands together. "And it's cold. I don't remember it ever feeling so much like a real Christmas."

"Where do you need the ladder?"

She wrinkled her nose. "I need to put the garland on first, then the lights."

"We have the lights and ladder. Why not get this done, then we can get the other stuff?"

She shook her head. "It needs to be done in the right order."

"It's Christmas decoration. How terrible can it be?"

She glared at him. "That's the problem. Sometimes you don't see the disaster until it's too late."

"Okay. So where is the garland?"

"It's in the building out back of the lumberyard."

"Let's go get it, then." He needed to keep moving. Looking at her was risky to his heart.

Hands in pockets, he followed her down the stairs and out the back door. "It's gotten colder again. Should I get the boys?"

"No. They'll be fine. Danica will bring them in if it gets too cold." The tall woodshed blocked the wind as they entered. Lumber was stacked two stories high, and in the back was a long workbench covered with greenery and red ribbons. The evergreen had to be thicker than his thighs.

Jackie pulled a wobbly flatbed cart to the table and started layering the green and red carefully across the wood planks.

"Let me help." He picked up one of the large wrapped bundles, but she stopped him.

"No. It's okay. I got this."

He stepped back and watched as she arranged each branch, ribbon and ornament as carefully as a good bull rider arranges his gear before a ride. "You like order."

She shrugged as if it didn't matter, but he sensed an underlying tension, one that stopped her from relaxing and enjoying life—even when everyone else was caught up in the joy of Christmas.

He looked around for something to do. "Why am I here?"

"Every small town needs a good-looking cowboy. I'm sure the tourists would love to meet a real hometown bull rider." She didn't even glance at him.

His jaw tightened. *Really.* "Yeah, that was my father's thought, too." The man had ignored him until he'd started making a name in the PBR circuit. All of a sudden he was good for business, and his father and uncle became his most prominent financial sponsors. "I'm going. Tomas needs to rest, and we still have a bunch of stuff to do at the ranch." He turned to leave.

"Max." She caught up with him before he made it outside. "I was just teasing. I didn't mean to upset you. Most people don't mind being called good-looking." She indicated her loaded cart. "Will you help me get this up the stairs? I'm afraid I'll drop something if I try to do it alone."

He saw concern in her eyes. Maybe pity. Now she thought he was oversensitive or had daddy issues. He was such an idiot.

Riding bulls was so much easier than dealing with life. He looked over her shoulder. He feared she saw the weakness in him. The truth of who he was.

He forced a smile. "Sorry, just worried about the boys. What do you need me to do?"

She directed him with the sureness of a drill sergeant, keeping watch over the cargo as he pulled.

"There's a platform attached to a pulley in the back of the store. We'll load the cart, then go upstairs to lift it."

Once they got the flatbed secure, she led him up the back stairs. In the corner of the newly restored room stood a huge iron wheel. It had to be at least eight feet tall.

"Crank here, and it will bring the cart up to us. Then we can unload."

"I've never seen anything like this." With her help, he started turning the large handle. The metal gears and chains creaked as the platform reached the second floor.

"This is a two-hundred-year-old elevator. I had wanted to refurbish it forever. One of my brothers-in-law finally got it working again a couple of months ago." She beamed like other women did over diamonds.

They wheeled the cart onto the balcony, where she had him hold the garland as she attached it to the columns and trim. She laid it a foot at a time, intertwining the lights as she went. He had never seen someone take Christmas decorating so seriously. "Do you do this every year?"

She kept on twisting the ribbon, her tongue between

her teeth. She was so focused on her job she hadn't heard him.

A smile pulled at his lips. As a teen, she had done the same thing whenever something had her full attention. Back then, he thought everything she did was fascinating. She still captivated him. She was so cute. Not that he needed to notice that. She'd made that clear yesterday.

With the last light perfectly placed, her gaze swung to him. "The last couple of years, everyone runs and hides when it comes time to decorate the storefront. I've been accused of being hard to work with."

"You? They just don't get how important the details are." He grinned.

"Exactly." She hopped down the ladder. Turning, she knocked a delicate tea cup off the edge of the table. In her rush to catch it, the cup broke and cut her palm. It hit the floor and shattered.

Blood spattered the white porcelain. Tremors rattled her hands. Her breathing became sharp and hard. She didn't move. Locked in place, she just stood there, looking down. The blood started dripping. "Jackie." He reached out to touch her, but she didn't acknowledge him. "Is there a first-aid kit?"

Her head shot up, eyes wild. "There's blood."

He scanned the area. Inside the door stood a roll of paper towels. Grabbing them, he applied pressure. "Once we get the blood stopped, we can see how deep the cut is. It's hard to tell with fingers. They bleed easily."

Her hands wouldn't stop shaking as he wiped at the blood.

She tried to pull free. "Don't worry about me. We need to clean the floor. There's blood and…" She made a noise that was somewhere between a sob and grunt. "Don't let Daddy see."

"Let's stop the bleeding first, then we'll clean up the blood. I promise the area will be pristine before anyone sees it."

Her breathing returned to normal, but he could still feel her rapid pulse. Another deep breath and she seemed to regain control. Her head remained down.

"There's a first-aid kit under the cabinet to the left." She pulled her hand free and stumbled inside.

He was right behind her. "I'll get it." Without another word, he quickly cleaned and wrapped the cut.

As soon as he let go, she gathered cleaning supplies and went back to the balcony. As the sun went down, so did the temperature.

"Jackie, are you okay?"

She nodded.

Something was off. Maybe being at the crash site had upset her on a deeper level. The past always had a way of messing with the present.

"I'm fine. I just don't like messes or blood." She fidgeted with the garland and ribbons she had already arranged several times.

"Is this about seeing the accident site yesterday? How old were you, four or five?"

"That has nothing to do with this. I should have never told you about that." She moved to the far corner of the balcony and stared out over the holiday festivities.

Pulling her sweater tighter, she wrapped her arms around her waist. "I was supposed to stay in the truck. When things aren't where they belong, someone gets hurt. Like that cup being too close to the edge when I wasn't paying attention." She scowled, then closed her eyes. "I know it's more complicated than that, but Daddy told me to do something and I didn't."

"You really should talk to him." He wanted to hold her, but the stay-back vibe was strong.

"If he found out now, what good would it do? It would make him feel worse. He doesn't need or deserve the guilt."

"But what about you? I'm not an expert, but I think you do need to talk to someone. It can't be healthy to hold on to something like this. You were a tiny little girl who saw something you shouldn't. I'm really the only person you've told this to?"

"I'm okay. Seeing the site for the first time caught me off guard. I never think about it anymore."

"Jackie, at least talk to your sisters."

"No. What's the point? It would just make everyone sad. It's in the past, right?" She made a dismissive gesture. "It's done, long buried. Bringing it up again will only cause more pain. My family's in a perfect place right now. New babies on the way. Even Daddy's dating. Everyone's happy."

He started thinking that sometimes the past did need to be dealt with. "What about you?"

She shook her head. "As long as they are happy I'm good."

Did she really think she didn't matter? Tears hovered on her bottom lashes. When he was younger he had wanted to slay dragons for her. Then he got smart and buried those stupid notions, right along with his writing. But those eyes had him wanting to be the kind of man who could fix all her hurts.

With a tight smile that broke his heart, she looked him in the eye. "I'm sorry. I don't know what's wrong with me. Maybe it's the holidays. Do you realize next week will be the anniversary of our mothers' deaths?"

"It's not an anniversary I keep track of. You don't have anything to apologize for. I'm out of line. I'm the last person to give family advice." He pointed at himself. "You know the *D* in Delgado stands for *dysfunctional*."

She snorted. "None of us are perfect."

He wanted to tell her she was just about as close as anyone he knew, but it sounded too much like a come-on. They stood in silence as the lights started to illuminate the main street. The courthouse became a winter wonderland, a million tiny twinkles bringing the stars to earth.

"Hey, Jackie!" Sammi stood below them, surrounded by the kids and her two other sisters. "Is the Bergmann building ready for Christmas?"

Leaning over the railing, Jackie smiled and her face lit up. "Y'all ready to flip the switch?"

A chorus of yeses filled the air.

"The gingerbread party is about to start, and the kids don't want to be late," Danica yelled at them.

He looked at Jackie. Why did he have a feeling he was about to find himself at another down-home Christmas tradition? "Gingerbread houses?"

She nodded as she moved to the doors. "Yes. For a donation, you get a house to decorate. The boys will love it, and you might have fun, too. The last few years it's become a bigger event. It's a fund-raiser for a couple of organizations in the county that help kids and families."

With one hand on the switch, she called down to the small crowd gathered below the balcony. "I need a countdown."

They all started counting. "Ten…nine…eight… seven…six…five…four…three…two…one…now!"

Suddenly he stood in the midst of radiant light, and it

wasn't all from the strings of bulbs they had hung over the balcony. Jackie's eyes reflected the joy that represented everything good about Christmas and family.

This is what every Christmas card tried to capture. Love, warmth and belonging.

He stepped back. He didn't belong here.

The grip she had on his hand caught him by surprise. Despite the cold, her touch was warm. Pulled along down narrow stairs, he was pretty sure this was how it felt to get sucked into Alice's Wonderland.

Chapter Eleven

❧

The smell of ginger and cinnamon stunned his senses. Like a bull charging, memories slammed into him: his mother, laughing, her dark hair pulled back; a lopsided gingerbread house with fat peppermint sticks propping up the porch.

He tried to grab the fading mental image. Did it really happen? He didn't remember making gingerbread houses with his mother.

He scanned the room. Several tables were covered with white paper and scattered with bowls of candy. There were so many children darting around he couldn't even begin to count them. He was sure he'd never seen this building before.

Maybe the last hit to his head had created false memories. Was that possible?

"You okay?" Jackie tilted her head, as if trying to figure him out. "I guess this is not your usual Saturday night?"

He shook his head, but it didn't help sort out the images in his brain. He took off his hat and pushed back his hair. "Do you see the boys?" He needed to ground himself. But something stirred inside him. His skin tightened.

"Maximiliano Delgado!" A small woman who filled her space with energy was hugging him before he knew what had happened. She moved so fast he hadn't seen her coming. She smelled like sugar cookies. He looked over the woman's silver-streaked bun at Jackie, hoping she saw the pleading question in his eyes.

"Rosa, how do you know Max?" Her forehead creased.

He was just as confused as Jackie.

"Oh, *mija*." She let go of him and hugged Jackie. "For the first eight years of his life, he spent every holiday here in Clear Water. His mother brought him into town to participate in the activities. She was one of the organizers of the gingerbread houses."

The older woman shifted her attention back to him. "You probably don't remember me. I'm Rosa Ortega. Your father was never happy about that, but then again your father was not a very happy person." She put her hand on his arm. "When we lost your mother, I had hoped he would bring you back after the accident. But you're here now, and you brought your brothers. That's a good thing. We all need family traditions. Your mother would be so happy to see this."

He had no idea what to say. Why didn't he remember his mom bringing him here? "Have you seen the boys?"

She smiled and pointed across the sea of laughter and color. "They are at the Bergmanns' table on the back row." She squeezed his arm. "Merry Christmas, *mijo*. Have fun. We'll see you and the boys at church Sunday?"

Not knowing how to respond, he found himself nodding.

"Why didn't you tell me your mom made gingerbread houses with you?" Jackie made her way through the throngs of happy people. A few had a smile for him, but most still eyed him with suspicion. Rumors of him selling to developers had spread faster than the thistle.

He kept his gaze locked on Jackie. She waved to people, greeting them by name. Then she looked back at him, her braid falling across her shoulder. That smile. Right then, he knew he'd never stopped loving her. The foundation of his world rocked.

"This is something I've done all my life. Never missed one. You know that means we met before that summer on the rodeo circuit?" She paused. "I always wondered—why didn't you tell me who you were when we first met in Bandera?"

"I did tell you."

She sighed and went back to walking. He just stood there. Had he met her when they were little? She was talking again, but he couldn't hear her.

Turning back around, she frowned. "It helps to get where you're going if you walk. What's wrong with you?" Taking his hand, she led him across the herd of people.

He never thought of his mother. Now he couldn't get her out of his head. He had been so mad at her for leaving him. He hadn't really understood what it meant when his father had told him she was dead. Frankie had said she had gone to sleep and would never wake up. For the longest time, Max had been afraid to close his eyes.

A gentle tug pulled him back to the present. "Max?" She stood next to him now, her fingers surrounding his in warmth. He looked up and slammed into her stare. Concern clouded her green eyes.

He tried to talk, but his throat was dry. He cleared it. "I don't have a lot of memories of my mother. Other than her not being there. I was angry about that before

I really understood that she hadn't abandoned me out of choice." His voice felt like it had to crawl through broken glass.

She squeezed his hand. "Oh, Max." Light reflected off her eyes. She was about to cry. "Do you want to leave?"

"No. I want to join the boys."

She tucked her arm around his. "I'm so sorry, Max."

"For what?"

"Your mother. A boy shouldn't lose his mother so young."

"You lost your mother that day, too."

She nodded. "But I had my father and sisters to help me through it. You were all alone."

They stopped at the end of a table. His brothers were laughing and passing bowls full of candy and other items for the houses they were decorating. He had been alone, but they didn't have to be.

Jackie gently pushed Isaac's hair off his forehead. "Hey, guys."

Isaac held his gingerbread house up. "Look, Max!" The joy on his face was contagious. He went back to constructing the little house. Tomas worked one-armed, his tongue sticking out. Ethan reached across to help him.

Jackie nudged him with her shoulder. "We probably did this together when we were little tykes."

"I didn't even remember until we walked in." What kind of son forgets the things his mother did with him? "The building doesn't seem familiar at all."

"That's because we used to do this in the fellowship hall, but it got too small." She studied him. "You really don't remember doing this?"

He shook his head. "I don't have many memories at all. My early childhood is a big black hole."

Her green eyes were full of pity. He looked away. Why did he tell her that? Now she felt sorry for him. He hated pity.

The exit wasn't far, but the boys were deep in candy and icing.

"Do you want a log cabin or Victorian?"

He blinked at Jackie, trying to decode her question.

"What type of gingerbread house do you want?" she added.

His pocket vibrated. With relief, he pulled out his phone. It was Vanessa. She was finally getting back to him. "I've got to take this. Will you keep an eye on the boys?"

"Of course. Everything okay?"

He nodded and headed out the door. The cool air was sharp against his skin. Hopefully, Vanessa was calling to let him know he could get back to his real life.

Jackie watched him go. Guilt left no room for joy. He didn't even have memories of his mother. And it was all her fault.

Tomas laughed as Ethan ate Isaac's front door. Jackie pulled herself back to reality. She needed to be in the moment, not lost in a past she couldn't change, no matter how much she wanted to.

Squeezing in between her nieces, she started organizing her candy by color and shape. Across from her, Ethan did the same. He was taking his time adding details to his cabin.

Concern in his dark eyes, Tomas looked up at her. "Where's Max?" Anxiety edged his voice.

"He'll be right back. Your aunt called him."

"Our aunt?" Isaac popped a handful of M&M'S into his mouth.

Jackie glanced at her watch. He'd been gone for a while. Some of the families had already packed up and were leaving. "Let me go check on him."

Max was just a couple steps outside the door, looking up at the starry sky.

"You okay?"

"It's amazing how different the sky is without clouds and no bright security lights."

She stood next to him and studied the open space. "I've always loved the night sky. My dad told me once that God put the stars in the sky to remind us that He is our light, even in the darkest times. If you move toward Him, everything else will fall into place."

Laughter and happiness floated from the community center.

"Do you believe that?" His voice was low, rough.

"Sometimes I forget. I like to pretend I'm in charge." She chuckled. "But when I focus on God, when I remember to live in my faith, the hardest moments become bearable."

He turned to her. "You seem to have it all together."

She took a breath, summoning up the courage to face him. His gaze had an intensity that made her fidget. Like he was searching for her secrets, and would find them. "I think we all have wounds or fears."

He took a step closer to her. "What are yours?"

His warmth called to her. She cleared her throat and glanced back at the door. "We're wrapping things up inside. Did you get good news from Vanessa?"

His attention returned to the dark sky.

She waited for him to continue, but there was just more silence. "Max?"

Hands in his pockets, he looked at his boots. "She's able to finish up early, so she'll be here before Christmas."

"The boys really want to stay through Christmas." Concern for the boys was the reason for the skip of her heart. Not her feelings for him.

"She's coming here to let them celebrate the holidays in Clear Water. The good news is she thinks the puppies are a good idea. They don't need me. They're better with her."

"That's a cop-out—they do need you." She bit back the anger that swirled through her. "You know as well as I do that they don't really understand what death means. And they want you. Ethan is here for no other reason than to be near you. I thought you didn't want to be like your father."

He flinched as if she had slapped him. Had she gone too far? Why did she care so much about him and the boys, anyway? It wasn't her place to mend this broken family. She had her own to fix.

"I'm a bull rider. And I'm getting older. I don't know how many rides I have left. This isn't forever, just a couple of weeks."

"Weeks that're important to your brothers. How could you do this to them?" She wanted to yell at him and ask why he was leaving. The pounding of her heart scared her. It wasn't good that she cared this much. It wasn't like they could ever be in a real relationship. She was just helping him so he would help her with the historical project. It was business.

Taking a deep breath and a step back, she nodded.

There couldn't be anything between them, no matter how much she longed to…ugh. No. Those kinds of thoughts had to be stopped now.

Her father always told her thoughts turned to words, which shaped your actions and that created your destiny. "I came out here to tell you that the boys are done. They want you."

He turned to her, then scowled. She wasn't as good at hiding her disapproval as she thought. "I'm not taking full custody of the boys. I can't." He brushed past her to go through the door.

"You mean you won't." *That was too far.* Following him into the community center, she lectured herself. His life wasn't her business. She needed to keep her opinion to herself.

She joined Max at the table with the boys.

"Those are great," she heard him exclaim. "I like the colors you used. Ethan, yours is so detailed."

The teen shrugged, but stood a little taller.

Max turned to Danica. "Is there anything they need to do before we leave?"

Jackie's twin shook her head. "They were great helpers." She lifted her phone. "Smile, boys. Max, get in the picture."

He stood behind his brothers. His smile was soft as he patted the boys on their shoulders. "Thank you for including the boys, Danica."

"They were so good. I can see why Jackie is falling for them." She helped the boys place their little houses in a box. "Y'all will be at church tomorrow, right?"

Tomas and Isaac both said yes at the same time. Isaac took Max's hand. "Our new friends will be there. Please."

His smile tightened. "There's too much to do on the ranch, and I've got to get some practice in if I'm going to be ready for the finals."

Don't do it, Jackie. Don't do it. She made the mistake

of looking at the boys. "I can come at sunup. You can take off and do what you need to do. Then we can head to church." The words *as a family* were left unspoken, but were in her heart. This was not good.

"I don't know." Max had the look of a man who had just walked out of a tornado.

"You don't have to come. I can take the boys to church. That will give you more time—" she twirled her hands in nervous circles "—to do whatever you need to do."

"Please." Tomas's plea was soft and hesitant.

With a defeated look, he nodded. Placing a hand on the boys' shoulders, he ushered them to the door. Before he reached it Rosa stopped him. She handed him something. A photo?

As Jackie reached his side, Rosa pointed to the little library off the lobby. "The church had years of photo albums. You and your mom are in many of them. Since you didn't remember doing this with her, I figured you didn't have any pictures of your own. Pictures are the best way to keep our memories."

Max just stared at the photo in his hand.

"I want to see!" Isaac pulled Max's arm lower and peered over. "Hey, that looks like me."

Tomas was on the other side. "That's not Max! That's Isaac." He squinted. "Or me, but I don't remember that. Who's the girl?"

Max's Adam's apple bounced. "That's my mom, and that's me when I was about your age."

His youngest brother's eyes were huge. "Really? We'll get as big as you when we grow up?"

Rosa laughed. "Maybe taller. His momma was a little bit of a thing. She was shorter than me. Maybe five feet tall. He's lucky to have reached six feet."

Max looked surprised. "Really? I don't remember her being that short."

She patted him on the arm and laughed. "You were much shorter yourself back then."

With a lazy pull of his mouth that almost looked like a smile, he made a grunt that could have been a chuckle. He held out the picture.

Rosa waved him off. "We have albums full. There are more pictures of y'all if you want to look at them sometime. I don't think there are any of your father. He never came around. But she wanted you to know your family history. She collected stories from the old-timers. She loved history. That's how your mothers became such good friends." She wiped her eyes on her flowery apron. "Well, enough of that old talk."

Max stared at the picture, like he didn't know what to do with it.

After hugging each of the boys, Rosa turned back to Max. She cupped her small hands around the hand that held the lost memory. "Take it. It's yours."

With lips torn between smiling and crying, Max nodded. "Thank you." After looking at it one more time, he tucked it away in his jacket.

Jackie had so many pictures of her mother, she couldn't imagine not having one. Plus, she had her father and sisters. His father had shipped him off.

Danica joined them. "I'll text you the pictures of the boys tonight."

"That would be great. Okay, guys. Are you ready to get your puppies?" He said it with a slight grin, as if he wasn't giving them the best news.

The boys froze. Eyes wide, they stared at Max.

Moving between the boys, Ethan pulled them close as

if to protect them. "You talked with Vanessa? She said okay?" Skepticism sat heavily in his voice.

With a big grin, Max nodded. "We can pick them up today."

"Yes!" they shouted as one. Even Ethan had a smile on his face.

"Hurry." Isaac wiggled on his feet. "I can't wait any longer, or I'm going to lose it."

Ethan held the box with their houses in it. "Too late. You already lost it." He grinned at his brother.

Tomas frowned as he followed his brothers out the door. "What did he lose?"

The brothers teased each other and laughed as Max walked beside Jackie.

"Ethan sure has come out of his shell in the last couple of days," she commented, trying to push away the guilt.

"You mean, he climbed out of his phone and joined the real world?"

"Just a few days ago he was surly and withdrawn. It's a shame he has to go back to Chicago."

"Jackie, don't. He has a mother and needs to get back to school. We both know that life isn't fair most of the time."

"But if you ask—"

"No." He huffed. "I have to get back into the circuit, and he needs to go home."

Picking up his pace, he moved ahead of her.

She couldn't stop herself. "But Isaac and Tomas…"

Over his shoulder, he shot her a glare.

Message received. "I'll see you in the morning."

Her promise to keep her opinions to herself hadn't lasted long. Just last Sunday, Pastor Levi had been talking about waiting for the Lord. Yes, she needed to learn to wait. Meddling in other people's business was not living by faith.

But, Lord, my heart hurts for Max and his brothers. What do I do with the desire to help compared to having faith and allowing God to work? What if Max isn't listening to God?

She really needed to get this meddling under control. No one needed a busybody in their life. Plus, she had already told Max a relationship couldn't happen between them. She had no right to tell him what to do. She had problems.

It was so much easier to point out other people's issues than to deal with her own.

Chapter Twelve

The house settled in around Max. After a messy bath full of bubbles and laughter, he had tucked the boys in and picked up the Children's Bible to read some chapters.

He snorted. The plan had been to put the puppies in their fancy little bed on the floor between the boys' beds, and he would read one story. The new bed went unused as the puppies snuggled under the covers with the boys, and he read four stories.

The clock taunted him with each tick. The boys had been asleep for a couple of hours. Max had tried to go to sleep, but after an hour of tossing and wrangling with the bedsheet, he came into the kitchen.

He ran his hand along the edge of the gigantic oak table. He didn't remember it ever being used.

His brain had gone into overdrive, digging up old memories. Yelling and fighting seemed to be the only thing his parents did together. What they fought about stayed out of his reach, but his name was thrown around several times.

He couldn't take his gaze off the picture in front of him. It was the only one he had of his mother. Ethan's mom had gone through the whole house, making sure every photo of the first Mrs. Frank Delgado was removed. Elbows on the table, he buried his fingers in his hair and closed his eyes.

The photos of his mother had been wiped out, then his poems and music. It felt like his father had been trying to erase him. But Jackie had found one of his boxes. He didn't remember hiding them.

What bothered him the most was forgetting his mother. How could he have forgotten her? Forgotten the time they spent together? Words banged around in his head, wanting out. Going to the old office, he found a legal pad and started writing.

His father wasn't here to lecture him about being a man. Even if he were, it wouldn't have made a difference. Max had spent his whole life trying to get one pat on the back, one lousy attaboy.

Why had it been so hard for his father to say he was proud of him, just once? That was all he'd wanted. What his father thought of him wasn't an issue anymore. Along with everyone else that he thought mattered, his father was gone. Just one more person who left him behind.

He tilted his head back. It should have never mattered anyway. He wasted so much time trying to prove himself to a man who didn't care. A stream of consciousness flowed across the blank page.

A muffled scream came from down the hall. It sounded like Tomas. Max rushed to the boys' bedroom and found the six-year-old sitting up in bed. Sobs made it hard for him to breathe, the small chest struggling to pull in air. The golden pup they had named Queenie licked his face. Isaac had climbed in to his brother's bed, too.

Sitting on the edge of the bed, Max pulled Tomas

against him. The superhero nightshirt was wet with sweat, even though it was cool. Small arms circled his neck, clinging to him as if his life was in danger.

"Shh, Tomas. I've got you. What happened?" He looked at Isaac for answers.

Tears ran down the five-year-old's face. He shook his head. "He wakes up crying sometimes. Something in his sleep scares him."

The boy's dark hair was sticking up in all directions. Max smoothed it down. "Tomas, I'm right here. Nothing's going to hurt you. Look, Queenie stayed with you. She already loves you." The puppy was putting its paw on the boy's leg.

The cries gave way to soft sobs.

"Can you tell me what frightened you? Do you have bad dreams?"

Against his neck, he felt Tomas nod. "Maybe it'll help if you tell me about it and we can pray." If he could help them find peace in faith, they could take that with them.

Isaac scooted closer, the black puppy tight in his arms.

"You were all gone. I was alone in the barn. The door was locked. I couldn't open it. I banged on it and screamed for you. Then water rushed in. I ran up the ladder."

"You were getting above the water. That was smart of you." Max felt so helpless as the small body shook. He could feel the fear. "It was just a dream, Tomas."

"But I could see you. Isaac, Ethan, Ms. Jackie, the puppies, even Momma and Daddy. You were all trapped in the water, and I couldn't get to you. I tried to grab someone's hand, but the water pulled you all down. I called for help, but no one could hear me. I was all alone." He started crying again. "You were all dead."

"I'm right here. So are Isaac, Queenie and Baby. Ethan is asleep in his room. Do you want to check on him?" A small nod was followed by a sniff. Standing, Max adjusted Tomas in his arms, then took Isaac's hand.

Ethan's door was cracked open. They all leaned in. Ethan lay on his back, one arm over his head and the opposite leg bent. A bare foot poked out from under the blanket. Max was a little startled to see the teen had the same sleeping habits as himself. "See, Ethan's safe in bed, sound asleep. Just like we should be, right?"

Backing out, he slowly closed the door. "Need to use the restroom?" They both shook their heads. "Okay then. It's time to go back to sleep. I'll read one story, then it's lights out."

The boys climbed into one of the beds, right along with the puppies. He finished the story, and they asked for another. "Guys, it's late and we all need to get some sleep. Morning is going to make an appearance soon." His eyes were finally getting heavy. With a yawn, he stood and stretched. "'Night, boys."

He didn't even make it to the door before they called him back. They went back and forth for a bit until Max got firm and told them to go to sleep. He would leave the hallway light on. As he stepped through the door, Tomas started crying.

Max turned around and saw Tomas sitting up. "I'm scared. Please don't leave."

"Oh, Tomas, there's not enough room in this bed for me."

Isaac sat up, a puppy in his arms. "Can we sleep with you?"

Max sighed. He had a feeling this was going to be the only way any of them would get some shut-eye.

It didn't take much time for the little herd of boys and puppies to make themselves comfortable in his bed.

It was a king-size bed, and it amazed him how much room four small bodies claimed. It didn't look like he was going to get much sleep tonight.

Jackie knocked. Bundling her coat around her, she peeked in the window beside the door. Where was everybody? Max always had the boys up by now. She got out her phone to call. He had told her to be here. Before she could find him in her contacts, she heard movement inside.

Peering in, she saw a disheveled Ethan making his way across the living room. His T-shirt looked two sizes too big. It had to be Max's. He opened the door.

"'Morning, Ethan."

His eyes were still closed, and his hair stuck straight up on the left side. He had never looked more adorable. She stepped into the living room. "Aren't your feet cold?" It was warmer inside. But the tile floor had to be freezing.

He looked down as if he didn't realize he was barefoot.

"Where're Max and the boys?"

He rubbed his eyes and shrugged. Squinting past her, he looked at the clock on the mantel. "Oh, man. I can't believe Max hasn't woken us up." He looked around like he just realized where he was. "I'll go check on the boys."

She followed him down the long narrow hallway.

"They're gone!"

"What do you mean, 'they're gone'?" She looked over Ethan's shoulder. The beds were a mess, but empty.

Ethan rushed into the room and threw back the blankets, then ran to the closet. "Where are they?"

"Probably with Max. Maybe they already went out to the barns to feed the animals?"

"Why would they leave me?" He stood in the middle of the room looking lost.

"You've been working hard. It's Sunday. Maybe he let you sleep in, or they're in Max's—"

He sprinted out of the room to the door at the end of the hall. He opened it and his shoulders sagged. Walking up behind him, she saw a bed full of arms, legs and puppies. They all seemed to be using Max as some sort of pillow. Her heart melted into one big gooey mess. Despite how he had been raised, he was a good man. If only he could see it.

She placed her hand on Ethan's back. "See, they're fine. I'll go to the kitchen and start breakfast. You wake up your family."

The coffee was done, and she had eggs and bacon cooking when the little band of sleepy brothers joined her.

Tomas and Isaac sat at the dining-room table in their pajamas, their eyes half-closed. The puppies sat right next to their chairs. Ethan peeled an orange and shared it with his brothers.

Jackie handed Max a cup of hot coffee. Leaning against the counter next to her, he held it with both hands. He took a sip and groaned with satisfaction.

"Rough night?" She wanted to brush his tousled hair with her fingers. It was better to stay focused on the eggs. With a quick motion, she slid them onto the plates she had lined up.

"Tomas had a nightmare." His voice was low, so she

leaned in closer. "The whole family, including you and the puppies, were drowning and he couldn't save us."

Her hand went to her chest. "Oh, no." She tried to breathe, but pressure pushed down on her lungs.

He put his hand on her shoulder. "Jackie?"

She shook her head and picked up the plate. Carrying it through to the dining room, she hugged Tomas and Isaac good morning before rushing back into the kitchen.

Those little boys who needed so much love. The love and comfort Max never got after the death of his mother. Was this God's way of letting her make amends? Giving her a second chance? She dropped her head and took a deep, steady breath.

Max put down his cup. "Are you all right?"

"Yes. No." She met his gaze. "After the accident, I dreamed I was in the car and knew what was going to happen, but I couldn't stop it. Sometimes my sisters and father would be in it, too. There were horrible details, blood and…"

"And you didn't tell anyone, did you?"

"No. I didn't want them to feel bad." *Or to know it was my fault.*

He pulled her into his arms, pressing his cheek against the side of her head. "I'm so sorry."

"The nightmares got worse after our stepmother separated me from my sisters."

"Separated you?" His fingers stroked her hair.

"She thought it was unhealthy that we all slept together. She said we needed to be able to sleep alone, so she locked us in our own rooms. Danica and I would sleep on the floor on each side of the adjoining door. I could hear her crying. I promised to do whatever I could to make her happy again. I've been an absolute failure."

"She seems pretty happy to me."

She shook her head and stepped back. It was difficult pulling away from his warmth and comfort. She focused on the landscape outside the window, keeping Max at her back, out of sight. "Not because of me. I did everything possible to keep her from Reid. I hate to admit it, but I was jealous. It really wasn't about her happiness. It was more about my selfishness and keeping my family close to me."

"There's nothing selfish about you."

He stood behind her, so close she could feel him breathe. All she wanted to do was lean in to his warmth and let him hold her. She was so tired of standing alone.

It would be so easy to let him hold her, but she would have to tell him the truth about their mothers.

He was leaving anyway. The rodeo was his calling. She didn't want to sit at home waiting to hear that he had been severely hurt. Plus, it would upset her father; she didn't want that. Jackie adjusted her hair clip and refocused her mind. "Sorry."

"You don't have to be sorry. I might be repeating myself, but you don't seem to be listening. You need to talk to someone."

"I'm good." She handed him his plate. "Here. Eat, then I'll get the boys ready for church. The first round of volunteers are ready to attack the old church this afternoon. Adrian thinks we can have it ready in time."

"Jackie."

"We have a great deal to get done before Christmas. You said you needed to get some practice in before you leave for the finals. That's coming up really fast." Without waiting for a response, she joined the boys. They made fast work of the meal, then took off to do their morning chores. Their laughter echoed down the hall.

A sadness tried to steal her heart. Standing at the sink, she stared out the window as the soft morning light coated the barns and arenas. God's love was in every stroke of His creation. If she kept her focus on God, she would be fine. No matter what happened. She had to believe that.

She needed to keep her distance from Max. He was leaving soon, and the boys would be gone. She pressed her palms against her eye sockets. It was too late to protect her heart, but she had dealt with loss before and she could do it again. The church could be done in two weeks if she stayed focused. She could do this.

Chapter Thirteen

Max ended the call from his uncle as he pulled up to the front of the old church. Tomorrow morning marked two weeks since Jackie started their morning ritual of arriving at his door while the sun still lingered under the horizon. It gave him a few hours of practice time before she headed off to the lumberyard.

She even managed a steady stream of well-organized volunteers working on the old church at all hours of the day. Every evening she was out there working on the project herself.

He wasn't sure when she slept, but it was paying off. He scanned the tall steeple and the well-manicured landscape. Even the road coming in from the highway had been grated and resurfaced. There was new life in the abandoned town.

The other building needed structural repairs before any work could be done, so all of her focus had been on the church. The church he was about to legally secure from his uncle. Letting her down had not been an option.

His uncle was happy with the outbuilding he had been sent, but he had still been stubborn about returning the old settlement to Clear Water. So Max offered him a deal he couldn't turn down. His uncle now owned 60 percent of the business, and Max had complete say on the ranch.

Somewhere along the line he had started sharing Jackie's vison. This was his brothers' legacy, too.

Jackie. She was in his thoughts much more than he liked. Any time he was close, she seemed to get away as fast as she could. He should have learned his lesson as a teenager. Wanting to be with someone more than they wanted to be with him wouldn't end well.

A group of men came out of the church and waved at him as they got in their trucks and drove away. Max slipped into the building. Layers of dust and grime had been wiped away, leaving polished wood and sparkling windows. Jackie stood alone by the altar, head bent as she concentrated on the work she was doing. Light traveled through the stained glass, highlighting her hair.

He leaned against the door frame and watched her. In this short amount of time she had worked wonders with her small army. She stood, arched her back and, chin pointing to the ceiling, stretched. After that she twisted at her waist, first to the right, then the left.

They made eye contact. For a mere second her eyes brightened but, just as quickly, her face tightened. Finally a smile settled on her face. A smile that lacked the warmth he wanted.

But then again, he had a nasty habit of wanting the things he couldn't have.

Wiping her hands on her jeans, she moved toward him. "Hey." She stopped a few feet away and crossed her arms. "I spoke with Joaquin this morning. Seems you two have been hanging out a lot lately."

"We've been getting on the bulls, and he's spotting me in my workouts." He still got mad when he thought of what his uncle had done. How could Rigo completely turn his back on his own son? At least his father had made sure his sons were taken care of physically and financially even if he didn't offer any of himself. His uncle had issues, but he always thought Rigo had been a good father. To his girls anyway.

"He told me you got the largest pastures burned and cleared of thistles." The silence became awkward.

"I spoke with my uncle." He had told himself to wait until he got the papers signed and delivered, but he couldn't hold back. He smiled at her, knowing this was one incredible Christmas gift.

She scowled at his grin. "About Joaquin?"

"No. As much as I'd love to have a talk with my uncle, Joaquin asked me not to. It was about the ownership of the buildings."

Hope flared in those twinkling green eyes. Then she pulled back, her expression closed. "Did he agree to give Clear Water the land and buildings?"

"No." He tried to keep a straight face, but his mouth twitched.

Her eyes narrowed.

"But he did agree to give me complete control of the ranch."

She yelled and threw herself at him. "You did it! You got the buildings!"

He took a step back and grabbed her upper arms to stay balanced from the force of her tackle. Everything went into her full-body hug. The citrus smell of her shampoo surrounded him. He wanted to hold her and never let go.

Gently he stepped back. "As soon as I get all the paperwork, we'll get a lawyer and make everything legal so my uncle has no say. The ten acres surrounding the church will belong to Clear Water."

Stepping back as well, she rubbed her hands along her arms, as if hugging herself. "You made it happen." There was a suspicious glistening in her eyes. "Our mothers would be so proud."

"You're the one that made this happen." His gaze swept the interior of the church. "This is amazing."

The joy on her face suddenly turned to concern as she looked behind him. "Where are the boys? They're not with you?"

"I have more good news." He tried to smile, but everything in him refused to acknowledge the happiness he should be feeling. "Vanessa is in town." He made the tight smile bigger. He was happy. This was good. Her arrival was just what he wanted. "She arrived early and drove straight to the house."

"Oh." Her expression looked as tight as his felt. "That's great news, right? Where are they?"

"This is her first trip to Texas, so they wanted to take her to Dairy Queen for ice cream. They gave me the job of getting you to join us for dinner. They want you to meet each other." And he was selfish enough to want to spend as much time with her as he could before he left.

"That's sweet of them. So, this is it? She's taking them?" She took another step away from him.

The urge to reach out and pull her back into his arms had to be beaten into submission. "Yeah, this is a great opportunity for me. I'll be able to get back sooner than I thought. The boys were talking her ears off about the pageant. They'll spend Christmas in Clear Water together."

"Without you. You're leaving?"

"I never said I was staying."

"Right. I know that." Her boots had her full attention. She looked up at him and those eyes burned a hole in his heart.

"I've gotten used to seeing the boys every morning. I'm going to miss them even more than I thought I would." Her throat convulsed as those green eyes started a rapid blink.

The battle to keep distance between them was lost. He took the five steps to her, and with his knuckle lifted her chin. He wanted to tell her that he'd never stopped loving her, but he had no right.

Soon he'd be gone, and she would move on to another project. Love and pain went hand in hand in his world. This was why he'd learned to stay detached. It was less painful. Not that his leaving was the reason she looked like she was about to cry. It was the boys she was going to miss.

"I'll make sure we spend every summer and winter break here." He looked at the large stained-glass window his family had commissioned so many generations ago. "This'll become our family tradition. But right now, I'm supposed to bring you home for dinner."

With a slight nod, she smiled. "Lead the way, cowboy."

Chapter Fourteen

Dinner had been an interesting affair. Vanessa asked the Delgado boys a million questions, but Isaac was the only one talking. The other three had gone mute. Even if Jackie gathered all their words, there still wouldn't be enough for a single sentence.

Ethan spent the whole time glaring at Max as if he had betrayed them. Tomas's gaze darted between Vanessa and Max, acting like he had been told to pick one and he couldn't. Max? She couldn't read him at all.

Vanessa had been a surprise. In her head, Jackie had pictured a cold sophisticated businesswoman, but she was warm and friendly. At the far end of the table, Vanessa had her head bent to focus on Isaac as he filled the dinner conversation with all the things they had done and wanted to do for Christmas. In turn their aunt told them how much there was to do in London and New York.

With dinner done, silence fell over the room. Jackie couldn't just sit there. If she thought about what was happening she'd start to cry. Standing, she gathered the plates.

Tomas pulled his puppy into his lap. "Are we still going to watch our movie tonight?"

"Of course." Max moved into the living room. "Ethan, why don't you and the boys get some popcorn, and I'll put in the movie." He glanced over his shoulder at the women. "We can sit on the front porch and talk."

On the porch Jackie settled in to the corner of the swing. She didn't expect Max to sit next to her, but he did. Close enough that she could feel his warmth. Vanessa took the rocker across from them. No one spoke as they sat back and took in the landscape. A small herd of white-tailed does crossed the pasture.

Vanessa wrapped her scarf tighter around her neck. "You have a very nice place. Will you be staying here between rodeo seasons? Is that how it works?"

"I'm not sure. The plan was to come in and get it ready for sale, but plans change."

She nodded. "That is too true. Did you know my sister was trying to convince your father to have you and Ethan join them for Christmas?"

He jerked his head away from the hills and frowned at her. "Why?"

"She wanted to mend your relationship. With him being so much older, she was getting concerned about the boys' futures. Since he was old enough to be their grandfather, Lynn was making plans for you to be in their lives if something happened to your father." She gave a dry chuckle. "Plans, right?"

"Yeah." He looked away, his lips in a tight line.

Jackie fought the urge to take his hand and reassure him that he could keep the boys if he wanted to. She wanted to offer to be there for them, for him. But it wasn't her place. So she intertwined her fingers, pressing them into her lap, and kept her thoughts to herself.

Max leaned forward and gripped the edge of the swing. His knuckles were white. "Speaking of plans, what are yours for Tomas and Isaac? They really want to stay here for Christmas."

She smiled at him. "I got that. That's not a problem. I canceled everything on my calendar so I could focus on the boys. After Christmas we'll head to London, and I'll get them settled there before I go back to work."

London? Her stomach pitched. She turned to Max. He couldn't let them go so far away.

He dropped his head. Not able to hold back any longer, she placed her hand on top of his and clasped their fingers together.

Lifting his head, he looked straight at Vanessa. "You're taking them to London? I thought you lived in New York."

"England is my new home base. I've contacted one of the most reputable nanny services in Europe. I have them on a waiting list for the best boarding school, and when Tomas turns eight, he has a spot there."

"What about Isaac? You're going to separate them in a couple of years? You can't do that."

"If I have custody of them, I'm going to do what I think is best for them. Routine and structure will help them adjust and feel safe. Besides, it's a great opportunity. They will get to develop connections with leading families in the political and business worlds."

Max pushed his hair back and stared at her. "Those boys need a family. They need each other, not networking and résumé building."

"It's only one option, and if I want it to be possible I have to get them on the list now. I'm not sending them away. The school is close to my place in London. But if I need to travel for business, their routine won't be disrupted. Listen, Max, if I'm taking full custody, I'm going to do what I think is best. If you want to make the decisions, then you can take them, but you can't have it both ways."

Max stood and walked to the railing. He put his weight on his braced arms. "They need more than just a reliable nanny and a nice bed. They need a family."

"If you feel so strongly about this, why don't you take them? They're my nephews, but they're your brothers. Lynn and Frank listed us both as guardians. My sister wanted you and Ethan in the boys' lives."

"I'm a bull rider with no wife. I'm not even in a relationship." His gaze darted to Jackie. "That's not a good life for the boys. I agree they need stability. But a boarding school?"

"I went to a boarding school. It's not a bad place."

He looked over the surrounding hills. "I can't picture the boys in a city. Maybe I could find a way to keep them."

Surprise caused Jackie to take a sharp breath. He might keep them?

Vanessa narrowed her eyes. "Max, this isn't a game. They need a permanent home. A schedule. I don't know much about the rodeo life, but I think you live out of a suitcase more than I do. I might not be there most days, but I can provide the boys with a good, safe environment. We can get together for the holidays. I always take those off."

Jackie moved next to him and searched his face. She could see the battle that was taking place in his heart. He loved those boys but...

"What if I want more than just holidays?"

"Max, if I leave here with the boys, I keep them. If you decide to be a full-time dad, there's no renegotiating. They need to know their future." She stood. "I'm here until Christmas. My assistant got me a cabin on the river. I'll be there if you need anything."

"Will you join us for church tomorrow? Tomas and Isaac will be singing."

"Church?" One corner of her perfectly colored lips twitched. "It's been a while."

"We can pick you up around ten thirty. The boys would like it."

"Okay." Her heels clicked on the concrete steps as she moved to her car. She paused and turned to him, rubbing the arm of her fitted wool jacket. "I messed up with my sister. She was thirteen when we lost our parents. I was twenty-three and just out of college. I made so many mistakes. I don't want to do the same with her boys. They need consistency and rules."

"Vanessa, I love these boys more than I thought possible. I want the best for them."

"They'll need more than love. Children need dependability and the security that they are taken care of every day." She smiled a very professional smile. "I'll see you in the morning." She climbed in to her rental, and they both watched until her taillights vanished.

"Max? Are you serious about keeping the boys?"

He shook his head. Doubt and confusion were written all over his face. "What am I doing? Everything I wanted is here, so why was I offering to keep the boys full-time?"

"Because they are your family and you love them."

"Family. I don't know anything about having a family, being part of a family. Not like you have. You're so close to yours. I don't know what to do. All the reasons I want to take Tomas and Isaac started overshadowing all the excuses I had for not keeping them." He tilted his head back and closed his eyes. "Could I be their father for the next fifteen to twenty years? Being a parent doesn't really ever stop. I don't think it should anyway." He turned to her. "Am I crazy?"

She laughed.

He raised a brow. "You think that's funny?"

"You asked me if you're crazy? You ride giant animals made of muscle, horns and hooves for a living. There's no doubt you're crazy. But are you out of your mind for wanting to keep your family together? You know how I feel about it, but you're the only one who can decide if you can do it. With God, I think anything is possible."

Slanting his head, he studied her. "You're one of the most honest and faithful people I know." He turned back to the house.

Honest and faithful? Ten tons of guilt just perched in her stomach. Not able to face him, she turned to the stars above. "I'm not so honest, but I'm working on trusting God more." She needed to tell him the truth, but now wasn't the time.

"Jackie, you trusted God to see you through all your hard times. You put your faith into action. And now the church will be ready for the Christmas pageant. I'm ready for the finals, and Vanessa is ready to take the boys. Everything I thought I wanted. So why do I feel so empty?"

"I don't know. You need to listen to God."

"Listen? How do you know what's God and what's fear?" He stuffed his hands in his pockets.

"God wouldn't leave you feeling empty. You have to be honest with Him and yourself." The word *hypocrite* bounced in her head. She really needed to change the subject. "Tomorrow afternoon is my last walk-through.

I'm putting up a plaque in memory of our mothers. I would like you to join me. It would be the two of us putting the final touch on their project."

Her heart beat a little faster. She was such a fraud. Why did she want things she couldn't have? She wanted to make them a family, but she didn't deserve them. She couldn't have them.

He opened the door and waited for her to walk into the house. "Yeah. I'll go with you."

A chill had taken over her body, and she didn't think it had anything to do with the weather. She was going to have to tell him the truth, and that meant she would lose him.

Chapter Fifteen

The wind rattled the window panes. Ice pelted the roof, tapping out a natural rhythm. Jackie ran her hand over the newly polished pew. Standing in the middle of the church, she could imagine a small congregation sitting close to keep warm as they worshipped, a fiddle and mouth harp playing the old spiritual songs.

Now that years of grime had been cleaned from the windows, the vibrant colors of the glass sparkled.

Despite the cold, darkening weather outside, warmth and comfort surrounded her. This afternoon they'd take the last step in this project—the plaque honoring the memory of their mothers.

Max surveyed the room. "So, everything's ready for the Christmas play?"

"Yes. But you already know that." He wouldn't meet her gaze. "Will you still be here?"

He moved around the room, touching the freshly painted trim. After a long silence, he sighed and leaned against the door to the side room. "Vanessa is here, so I'm sticking with the plan to be in Vegas."

"You're not completely healed. And what about the boys? They want you here."

His jaw flexed as he pushed away from the wall. He stood in front of one of the windows. "What they want and what they need are two different things. I've thought about it long and hard. This is the right move for me to make for all of us."

He moved as far from her as he could to below the largest window in the building, the stained glass one behind the altar.

"Max. Those boys need you." She wanted to reach for him, to tell him that she needed him, too. She moved to the edge of the aisle, but stopped short of approaching the platform. "Running won't fix the problem." She might be the worst hypocrite.

He didn't even look at her. Instead, he crossed to the front door.

"Max, you don't have to leave the same legacy as your father."

"Is this where you want the plaque?"

She nodded. Each tap of the hammer vibrated in her heart. If she was going to tell him the truth, she needed to do it now. He stood back and looked at the names on the wall, the names of their mothers.

He tilted his head and pushed something with his boot. Then dropped to his haunches. The boards beneath him got his full attention.

She stepped closer. "What are you doing?"

With a quick glance at her, he pointed to the tools they had been using earlier. "Hand me a flat head."

Crossing the room, she grabbed it and then went down next to him. "Did you find something?"

"Look. It's a different wood." With just a flick of his wrist, he dislodged the board.

She gasped and leaned closer to him. "What is that?"

He pulled up two more wide boards. "Steps." He looked at her. "Seems your church has a basement."

She shook her head. "They didn't have basements in this part of the country. The rock was too hard to dig through."

He stood and moved to the opposite side to remove more boards. "Well, then, I guess this is a room under the church. Which I believe some would call a basement." He lay flat on his stomach and stuck his head in the dark space. "It's small. Looks like storage." He pulled his legs under him and sat up.

Peering in, Jackie couldn't see much but cobwebs, old wood and rock. "Those steps don't look safe."

He scooted to the edge of the opening and dangled his feet over. With a grin, he tested the top step. "It's not deep at all. Even if the boards bust under my weight, I don't have far to fall."

"Maximiliano Delgado. You will not go down there until we can make sure it's safe. Not just the rotten boards, but there could be snakes, spiders and all sorts of other creatures in there. Then I'll be stuck dragging your body out."

"You're strong. I have no doubt you will be able to rescue me."

"But if you don't go in, I won't have to save your hide."

He ignored her. Bracing his arms on the edge of the boards, he lowered his body into the dark hole in the floor. His biceps strained as he moved slowly, testing the steps.

"Let me at least get a flashlight."

"You are no fun at all. I'm sure you made everyone take turns on a trampoline, one at a time."

Clicking the utility light on, she went back to him. He was standing on the steps now, his full weight on them.

"Do you know what can happen when more than one person jumps on a trampoline?"

He just snorted and shook his head.

She flooded the space below the church with light. Among the natural debris were jars and metal boxes. Max continued to descend until his shoulders were below the flooring. He held out his hand. "Give me the light. It's more of a crawl space than a room."

She lay down on her stomach and studied the space. "It looks like a small cellar." A box in the corner caught her eyes. "Is that a cedar chest?"

Stooping, he walked over to it. "It's locked. I think I can lift it."

"Careful." The mess he was walking through sent a shudder up her spine and down her arms. "Maybe I should clean it out first."

"Jackie, I ride thousand-pound bulls. I think I can handle a few—" he grunted "—cobwebs. Take the light, and I'll hand you the box. It's not that big."

Sitting the flashlight on the edge of the opening, she took the small chest. Thick leather straps wrapped its cedar sides. Her pulse surged. This was real history. A piece of the town's past.

He pulled himself out of the dark space. He crouched next to her and grinned like a pirate retrieving his treasure.

This was the boy she had fallen in love with so many summers ago. For a moment, she got lost in his gaze. What could have been if she hadn't…

Looking away from him, she focused on the box. About two feet long and a foot tall, it couldn't hold much.

He squinted and leaned closer. "Look. Two names.

Santiago Delgado and…" He dusted off some of the layers of dirt. "Annabelle—" He jerked his gaze back to her. "I think it says Bergmann. And a date. 1894? Maybe."

"Annabelle?" She ran the family history through her head. "I think that's my great-great-grandfather's oldest sister."

He looked at her as if she had just spouted the formula for a moon landing.

"What? I've spent a lot of time with my family history." Lowering her head, she cut off eye contact. "History is important."

"I think you prefer being in the past with people long gone to hanging out with people here and now."

"They are safer. I know how the story ends." Careful of the aged hinges, she lifted the lid. A cold draft went through the room.

He stood. Was he leaving? He picked up her coat from the pew. "It's getting colder." He opened the sturdy jacket and placed it around her shoulders.

Grateful, she focused on the inside of their treasure. "Look, Max! A diary. You read Spanish. I just know a few words and phrases." She ran her fingertips over the worn leather.

"This could be a primary source that gives information about our history. It could answer some questions." Swallowing, she looked up at him. "Not just the town's, but our families'. Annabelle was a bit of a scandal. She had a son but was never married. Why is her name on here with a Delgado?"

"Great. The Delgado men have a long history of abandoning women. Looks like we can add one of your ancestors." He sat on the closest pew. Elbows on his knees, he leaned forward. "I don't know about this. Maybe we shouldn't read it. Isn't it enough that my mother caused your mother's death?"

A gasp escaped before she could stop it. She bit her lip and looked out the window. The little bit of daylight was fading. "It wasn't your mother's fault." Her voice didn't sound like hers. It had become such a deeply ingrained secret that the words stuck in her throat. She should tell him the truth. But it wouldn't stop here with Max. Her family would be affected.

"Sorry. I shouldn't have said that." He stood and walked to the window.

A shiver sprinted down her spine, but it had nothing to do with the cold. "It wasn't your mother's fault." Acid burned her stomach.

Turning, he leaned against the window. "That's sweet of you to say, but we know that is not what the town believes. My mother crossed a bridge that had ice on it. Your father made it very clear where he stood at the time, and his opinion of the Delgado family hasn't improved over the years."

This was the perfect opportunity to tell him that the accident was really her fault. That his mother was innocent. She gently turned a page. An old piece of paper fluttered down. She lightly picked it up, and her pulse jumped. "Max! I think this is a marriage certificate, between Santiago and Annabelle."

"Are you sure?" He joined her on the floor. "You said she never married."

"Not according to family records, but..." She turned the pages of the small diary. "What does this say?"

He sighed. "Come on, it's getting dark. The last thing I want is your father gathering a posse to come rescue you." He looked at his watch. "Plus, Vanessa might need her own rescue. It's about time to feed the boys."

Her fingertips traced the delicate script that floated across the yellowed pages. "This belonged to your family. Maybe it was your family that was wronged. Don't you want to know?"

He extinguished the stove, ensuring it was out before he returned to her. With a sigh he held out his hand for the book. "I'm fine not knowing, but if it's important to you…" He took the fragile book and opened it to the first page. "The old script is a little hard to read. The diary belongs to Maria Delgado, Santiago's younger sister. She wrote this to…to right a wrong."

She moved closer to him. "But why are the book and license hidden here in the church?"

"Good question." He scanned the pages, his lips moving, but he didn't say anything.

"Max?"

"Oh, sorry. This isn't easy for me to interpret." He glanced at her, a scowl on his face. "Are you sure you want to know what she wrote?"

"Yes!"

"The families had forbidden the young couple to marry. Maria helped them run away. They got married in San Antonio. On their way back, the Bergmann men caught them." He looked at her. "She says they whipped Annabelle with a leather strap. When Santiago tried to stop them, they dragged him into the woods. No one ever saw him again."

She gasped. "They killed him?"

"She seems to think so. What a mess."

"A secret over a hundred years old and it still poisons the community."

He shook his head as he read more. "But the townspeople blamed the Delgado family for everything."

With a nod, she moved toward the door and away

from the man she was falling in love with. Who was she trying to lie to? He had her heart already. Was she destined to love a man she couldn't have?

"Max?"

"Yep."

"It wasn't your mother's fault." She took a deep breath. "I caused the accident."

At first, she didn't think he'd heard her. He set the book in the pew, then looked at her. "You were a little kid. You weren't even in the car. So why are you taking the blame for their deaths? You know that's ridiculous, right?" She didn't see the hatred she'd expected, just confusion.

She stared at the floor. "I had left my horse in the car. It slid under the brake, and your mother couldn't stop."

He closed the space between them. With one finger, he lifted her face. "Jackie, look at me." He waited until she brought her gaze up to meet his. "It was an accident. There is no way it was your fault. Does your father blame you?" The scowl deepened the V between his eyes.

"No. No. He doesn't know."

"Jackie." He cupped her face, his warmth battling the chill that was taking over her body.

"I haven't told anyone."

"Not even your sisters?"

She shook her head.

"The nightmares. The need to put everything in order. Have you been punishing yourself for something that you had no control over?"

"You're not listening. The day before the accident, Daddy told me to put my toys away, or someone was going to get hurt. I didn't feel well, so I didn't. The next day our mothers were killed."

"Oh, Jackie." He pulled her into his arms. "That's too much for one little girl to hold on to."

The tears started. There was no stopping them now. The cold slipped past her coat. Pulling back, she wiped her face with the back of her sleeve.

Max pulled Whataburger napkins out of his coat pocket and gave them to her. "You know, there would be a police report. Have you asked your father about the cause? Even if, for some bizarre reason, it was your toy, no one would blame you. They love you. Your family is one of the most loving, supportive group of people I've ever met."

"You make it sound easy."

"It's not easy. My faith is newer than yours, but there are a couple of verses I cling to for reassurance. One is from Philippians—we need to forget our past and look forward to what lies ahead. I struggle with that every day. Looking forward and trusting God. I have to remind myself that He is in control."

A sad attempt at a snort escaped her throat. "I might struggle with that one."

His lopsided grin lightened her heart. "You might?"

"How can you not hate me?"

He cupped her jaw, his thumb caressing her cheek. "You really thought I could ever hate you?" He leaned closer.

Before he could kiss her, she turned away from him, walked out of the church and climbed in to his truck. He followed with the box. After settling their treasure in the back, he sat behind the wheel, waiting for the heat to kick in. "You do realize childhood memories aren't reliable?"

"I know what I remember. My father's pain, my mother's blood. I was there."

"If that had happened to one of your nieces, what would you want them to do? Could they talk to you about it?"

She dropped her head to hide the tears.

A warm hand nudged her wrist, then Max intertwined his fingers with hers. He didn't say another word, just held her hand as they drove along the road that connected their families to so much tragedy.

Sharing her worst secret had not been the end of the world. Maybe it was time for her to grow up and be honest with her family.

Chapter Sixteen

The boys were excited about the box. Even Vanessa was interested. Apparently, she was fluent in four languages and experienced in translating. She trailed her finger along the fancy script. "Maria was hiding in the church when the couple was separated. Later, when she heard that Annabelle was expecting, Maria wanted to take the proof of their marriage to the Bergmann family to show them the truth, but her father wouldn't allow it."

Ethan frowned. "That's so wrong. The whole town blamed him for abandoning her, but her family killed him and dumped the body." He shook his head. "Why didn't her father want people to know that was his grandson?"

"I'm sure it had to do with inheritance. Annabelle's son, a Bergmann, wouldn't be able to claim Delgado land if he's not a Delgado."

"Wow." The teen shook his head. "That sounds like a Delgado move."

"Not all Delgados." Max frowned. Carefully he put the book back in the box. "Maria wanted the truth told." He smiled at Jackie. "You get to help her right this wrong. A few generations late, but the truth will finally be on record."

Vanessa shook her head. "I had no idea there was so much drama in small towns."

"Sometimes I think there's more, because there are limited forms of entertainment," said Jackie. "Max, this belongs to your family. Do you have a problem with me taking it to the county museum and library?"

"No. I'll put it in your car."

Ethan rubbed his hands together. "It's my turn to make dinner. Tomato soup and grilled cheese are on the menu. Vanessa is staying. Do you want to join us, Jackie?"

Her gaze darted from the box to Max. "I'm not sure."

He lifted the box and headed out the front door to her car. The wind bit into his skin. He should've put on his coat.

Being careful with the aged wood, Max secured the chest in the back seat. He closed the door and turned, startled to find her standing right behind him.

"Max. Thank you so much for everything you've done…and for not hating me."

"I didn't do anything. And you haven't done anything wrong. You're amazing, you and your determination. I feel sorry for anyone that gets in your way. I have no doubt it will all go as you planned."

Several emotions crossed her face. Emotions he couldn't read.

Her green eyes were darker. He could hear her breathing, feel it on his skin.

Pushing his hair off his forehead, she traced his jaw. "I don't to talk about you leaving. I think I'm going to kiss you, so if you don't want me to, you'd better speak up now." She looked straight at him. As though she was the only one who ever saw him.

Max wanted to tell her that he was hers. He always had been.

That was his first thought, but that was dangerous. He shrugged, hoping to hide the rapid beat of his heart. He had too much at stake to open up to her again. It might have taken a while but the lesson had finally stuck. He wasn't important enough to fight for.

Jackie would walk away, again. Like everyone else in his life. He would end up alone, but for a moment he could pretend he was hers.

Time stopped as she stood there, not moving closer but not backing away. Maybe she had changed her mind. He wasn't going to be the one to give in this time.

He was tired of not being good enough. He took a step back.

"Max?"

She was still waiting for his permission?

He stood still. She would have to come to him. He knew he was being petty, but this was for his teenage self, the one who'd thought he had someone who loved him until she'd walked away. It was a lie to tell himself that she was just another woman in his life, but it was a lie he needed.

She took a step closer, then leaned in to him, her lips softly leaving a trail along his cheek. He savored the sweet tenderness of her touch. Her hands moved from his elbows to his shoulders, pulling him closer. An over-whelming tide of warmth had him wanting to hold on with everything he had. He wanted more, but knew he couldn't have it.

Her movements became stronger, strong enough to put holes in the defenses that had taken him too long to build. With each heartbeat wild horses ran through his veins. He was past pretending she didn't matter.

This was the reason all other kisses had left him empty. He had been waiting for her. Gradually her grip softened, and she rested her forehead against his ear. The braid at the base of her neck tempted his fingers to loosen the strands.

Her hands caressed his shoulders and along his arms. They stopped at his wrists. "I'm not sorry I did that."

"That's good to know." What if he stopped thinking and just went with the moment, the feelings?

He wanted everything: her heart, her life, her family. He wanted all of it. "Kiss me again." He turned his head and nudged her. When he ended up alone later, he didn't want any regrets.

He was tired of being detached from life, of standing out in the cold, alone.

Lips against her ear, he tried to keep the yearning out of his voice. "Kiss me like I matter." The words were as broken as his heart. He wanted to take them back. He hated the weakness he heard in his own voice.

She leaned in and pressed her lips against his.

They weren't kids anymore, but adults with life experiences. For years, he had played this scene in his mind when he didn't have anything else to occupy his brain.

The fear dug in. The fear that a million kisses wouldn't be enough, that he wouldn't be enough. He dropped his hands, and she slid her fingers across his arms until her fingers interlocked with his.

"Stay." In his arms, in his life. He wasn't ready to lay out his heart that much, but maybe…

Each beat of her heart was visible in the little dip by her collarbone. Pulling away, she smiled up at him. One last light kiss on his cheek, then she squeezed his hands and turned away.

For a moment, he couldn't comprehend what was happening. She was leaving?

Frustration replaced longing. "You can't kiss me like that and then walk away."

She stopped but paused before turning around. "I'm sorry. I promised Dad I'd be home for dinner. It's already late. I want to talk to him about the box."

"What about us?"

"Are you still planning to leave in two days?" Her gaze scanned his face, looking for something.

His jaw popped. "That's the plan." Plans could change. All she had to do was ask him to stay.

"Then I'm not sure what there is to talk about." Her phone pinged, and she glanced down. "That's Daddy. I've gotta go. Bye, Max."

Her back to him, she started talking to her father. Just like the first time she left him standing alone. He was done being an afterthought in everyone's life.

Her SUV disappeared down the long drive. Tonight he thought they had connected more deeply. So why was she hightailing it out of his life? But the why didn't matter. He was done.

"Max!" Tomas opened the screen door. "It's cold out here! Is Jackie coming in for dinner?"

Max followed his brother inside and closed the door with more force than necessary. "Nope. She had more important things to do."

Chapter Seventeen

Max bent forward so he could look out the little oval window on the airplane. As they descended over Las Vegas, he could see the ornate and flashy strip calling to its visitors. He had worked hard to get here.

He rolled his shoulder. It had not been easy but success was his. He was back in the game. Closing his eyes, he hit his head on his seat. So why was the hollow feeling of defeat making him feel like a loser?

"Daddy, look. We're going down." The little boy in the middle seat stretched his neck so he could see. "Will Mommy be there?"

"Yep. She's waiting at the airport right now." The man patted his son's leg. "We're almost home."

Max's heart twisted, and he swallowed hard. It hadn't even been a full day and he was already missing the boys. Were they missing him?

His Bible was tucked into the pocket in front of him. Pulling it out, he flipped through the pages until he found the one he had highlighted in church last Sunday. He recalled Pastor Levi's words about listening to God. *Every morning we wake up and make a decision on which path we will take that day. One that takes us closer to God or a path we are trying to forge on our own.* He had been whacking at weeds, working hard to make his own way.

Proverbs 4:18. *"But the path of the just is as the shining light, that shineth more and more unto the perfect day."* Lifting his head, Max stared out the window. The sky was wide and clear. A backdrop of brilliant blue was spotted with a few white clouds. The sun's light radiated from behind.

God had already told him. But he had allowed fear to stop him. Fear fed into the lie. That he wasn't good enough. That he couldn't be loved. That he had nothing to give.

Why was he so willing to believe the lie? Fear and selfishness. He was protecting his heart at the expense of his brothers. He dropped his head and read the passage again.

Dear Father, You know my weaknesses, my hurts. I ask for forgiveness and offer forgiveness to those that hurt me. Tilting his head back, he savored the peace that flooded his nerves.

Tapping his arm, the little boy next to him smiled with a twinkle in his eyes. "Are you going home, too?"

His Adam's apple doubled, blocking any words. Why was such an innocent question bringing him to tears? "No, but I will be soon."

First, he would have to go to Dallas.

Jackie stared out the window. A thunderstorm had rolled through the valley this morning. The smell of fresh earth washed clean with the rain might be better than coffee and bacon. She took another sip of coffee. Maybe.

Max had left for Vegas two day ago, and she had been too much of a coward to go tell him goodbye.

After the stupidity of that kiss, she didn't want to risk doing something even worse. Like begging him to stay. He was back to his life on the road. The life he wanted.

Vanessa had the boys, and they would be leaving for New York after the pageant, then going on to London. Her chest ached. She closed her eyes, trying to block the pain. They would be a whole other world away.

She wasn't sure how it happened, but the Delgado boys had ended up with a big chunk of her heart.

Danica sat at the table, Reid close behind. Her sister looked a little pale.

"You feeling okay?"

"The morning sickness seems to be hanging around for lunch."

Reid went to the pantry. "You want some crackers and crushed ice?"

"That would be great." Danica put her head down and the girls twirled around the kitchen.

Jackie watched as Reid took care of Danica then settled the girls down to eat. Images of Max in a fatherhood role flashed through her imagination. She had always pictured her children being dark haired. Like Max.

"Are you heading to the church early?" Reid's question pulled her back to reality.

"Yeah. As soon as we finish lunch." She loved being around her family, but right now she felt a little raw. Max had chosen the rodeo over having a family.

Her father rushed into the room. Putting his coffee on the table, he grabbed his jacket. "There's a fire on the east side of the Delgado place on Herf Road."

Jackie stood. "That's where the church is."

"I know. I'm heading out. You want to go?"

She was at the door without answering. Her father had always been a volunteer firefighter for the county. At times she would go with him.

As they sped to the ranch, she tried not to imagine the worst. It had been safe all these years. There was no way she would lose it to fire now. Turning in to the new entrance, her father slowed down a bit, his body stiff and his jaw harder than normal.

They were going to drive past the site of the accident. Her father's white knuckles indicated that he was all too aware of that fact. Guilt crushed her. He had avoided this area since that day so long ago.

"Daddy." Her throat closed. She coughed. "I have something I need to tell you."

His frown went deeper, harsher.

What was she doing? This was not the time or place. She looked back at the site of the demolished bridge. There was never a right time. *One deep breath.*

"Sweetheart, you're scaring me."

Her stomach pitched. "It was my fault."

He glanced at her, his face marred with confusion. "The fire?"

Her nails bit into the skin of her palms. "Mom's accident." She rushed forward, out of breath. "I left my horse in the car after you told me to put it away. You said someone could get hurt and you were right." She swallowed a sob. "I saw it there at the crash site."

All of the color drained from his face. He hit the brake and looked at her. "You saw the crash site from the truck?"

"No. I followed you. I saw you holding Momma. I heard you." She shook her head. "I ran back to the truck, so you wouldn't see me. I'm so sorry."

"Oh, baby." He reached out his hand. It shook. Placing her palm against his, he gripped her fingers. "It had nothing to do with a toy. They hit a patch of ice and went into a spin. Right off the edge of the bridge. There were skid marks, so she had hit the brakes. It had nothing to do with you." He put his head down. "It was a horrible accident. Horrible. You thought it was your fault all these years?"

"If it was an accident, why do you blame the Delgado family?"

"Max's mother wasn't from Clear Water, but when she came to town with her husband and son, she wanted to return the old town to the county. No one wanted to work with her. There were the long-standing grudges against the Delgados, so old we'd forgotten most of the reasons."

He placed his hand on the back of her neck. "You're so much like your mother. She joined forces with Gabby Delgado, despite my objections." A slight pull at the corner of his mouth indicated a grin. "Or maybe because of them. That woman could be stubborn, but she had to be to put up with me. I…I lost my heart that day. It was easier to blame the Delgado family than myself or God."

Jackie nodded. A tear slipped past her eyelashes and landed on her father's wrist. "I thought my toy slipped under the brake, like it did the day before."

"No, baby. In no way was it your fault. We have enough pain and loss without adding to it. I'm so sorry I…didn't notice. I should have had you in counseling, but you were so young, I didn't think." He bit down hard on his lips, and moisture gathered at his lashes. "I've let you and your sisters down in so many ways." He kissed her forehead. "I wouldn't have survived without you girls. Y'all became my reason for waking up in the morning." He shifted gears and moved the truck past the river.

"I'm so sorry, Daddy."

"You have nothing to feel sorry for. I know I'm not good at saying I love you."

"I've never felt unloved." She leaned over and kissed his cheek.

Rounding the corner, they saw flashing lights through the trees and smoke rising behind the old church. Cutting the engine, her father turned to her. "Promise me you will let this go." His big hand cupped the whole side of her face like it had when she was little. "I can't bear the thought of you feeling any guilt over this. Please."

She nodded.

"I love you, Daddy."

"Love you, too, baby girl." With that, he ran to join the other volunteers.

The fire had been beaten back from the church. It hadn't gotten within a hundred yards of the old buildings. Jackie wasn't sure what to do. Glancing around, she spotted the ambulance. There was someone sitting in the back.

Rushing over, she came to a sudden stop when she saw the man Brenda was working on. She shook her head. It couldn't be. He was in Las Vegas.

"Max?"

"Oh, Jackie. I'm so sorry." Black soot and dirt was smudged across his face.

"What are you doing here?" Still confused, she stepped closer. That's when she saw his arms and hand. "You're hurt! What happened?"

"I decided to come back. I didn't want to disappoint the boys and…well, I wanted to see you. We never did have that talk. I came out here to talk to God. I saw the fire and called 9-1-1."

"He also tried to put out the fire by himself." Brenda was applying cream to his burns.

She glanced at Brenda. "Is he okay?"

"Minor burns on his left hand and both arms. Mostly first-degree, but you'll need to keep an eye on them. They can get worse. It's enough to keep him off a bull for now." The EMT moved past her. "I need to check on the others. You stay here and don't touch anything."

Max tried to look around the ambulance door. "Have they contained the fire?"

"I don't know." The fire wasn't what was occupying her mind right now. "Why are you here?"

"I was trying to stop the fire from—"

"Not in the ambulance. Why are you back in Clear Water?"

He grunted as though that question was too hard to answer. She put her hands on her hips and stared him down.

He looked down at his hands. "I discovered what I needed most was being here in Clear Water." He brought his eyes up to meet hers. "I realized God had given me some of the greatest gifts, and I was an idiot for walking away from them. The boys needed me and, like you said, I don't have to be my father. I want to make new family traditions."

Blood rushed in her ears. "What about the finals?"

He gave her his heart-melting, lopsided grin. "There's always next year. I have time to fully recover and have another go at it—" he shrugged "—or not. I came back for the boys." His Adam's apple bounced. "I want to spend more time with you, too."

"Me?" She pressed her hand against her chest, hoping to steady her breathing.

With a quick nod, he leaned forward. "Jackie, I love you."

She blinked, not sure she'd heard right.

"You don't have to say anything. But I want you to know it's not that teenage first love, but a love so deep I didn't even know…" His hand came up, toward her, but then he dropped it. "It's the kind of love that challenges me to be a better man. A man that deserves your gifts. A man of God that will stand and fight for his family."

He looked away from her, his gaze going to the smoke billowing above the trees. "But I think I might have messed up. We must have left one of the pasture fires smoldering from the thistles purge." His gaze met hers. "I'm so sorry. The church was almost—"

Stepping forward, she cupped his face and shook her head. "It was an accident. Just an accident." She gave a very unladylike snort. "Ironically, my father just used those words with me. I told Daddy my secret."

His eyes searched hers. "You did?"

"They hit a patch of ice. It was a horrible accident. My father hates talking about it—he never does—but he did for me. He told me to let it go." With her thumb, she wiped at the skin around his eyes. "You're a mess."

He turned his face and pressed his lips against her palm. She stepped closer and leaned her forehead against his. "Max, you tried to put the fire out before anyone got here. Don't do that again. These buildings are not worth your life."

"I'm not sure my life is worth much without you in it."

Her heart skipped a beat.

"Jackie. I want to raise the boys here in Clear Water. I wa—"

Her eyes went wide. "Wait. This means you're taking full custody of the boys?"

"Yep. When I landed in Vegas I knew what I wanted. I got on the next flight to Dallas and met with my uncle and one of the company lawyers. The ranch officially belongs to me and my brothers. I want to build a home and family here on my ancestors' land. I pray I don't mess those two boys up."

"You won't any more than other parents do anyway. You've got this."

"It'll take lots of prayers and maybe a bit of professional counseling, but we'll get through it as a family."

"What about Ethan?"

He nodded. "We're trying to see what we can work out with his mother. She's hard to read. For now, he is with us until his new semester starts mid-January. If she won't let him move down here full-time, he'll be able to come down once a month and holidays."

She brushed his hair back, noticing some of the tips were singed. "You're going to make a great father. Those little brothers of yours are blessed to have you."

"You're the blessing. I love you. I've loved you for a very long time. I want you to be part of our family."

Leaning forward, she pressed her forehead against his and wrapped her arms around his shoulders. "I don't know what to say. I—"

"Jackie?"

She jumped at the sound of her father's voice. Straightening up, she stepped away from Max.

Her father cleared his throat, then started coughing.

"Daddy, are you okay?"

"Yeah, yeah." He waved her off. "They have the fire under control. Lightning hit a tree. Max must have been right on it as soon as it started. The fire was contained due to Delgado." His attention focused on Max. "You going to be okay?"

"Yes, sir. Looks like I'll have to sit out this round of finals, but I got more important things to do anyway."

"So, are you—" he gestured between them "—an item now?"

She laughed. "'An item?' Really, Daddy."

"Isn't that what they call it now?" He lifted one eyebrow at her before turning back to Max. "I heard you'd been hurt fighting it on your own. Thank you. We both know how important this project has been to her."

Max looked straight at her father. "And she's important to both of us."

"Yes, she is." He narrowed his eyes. "Will you be at the pageant?"

"Wouldn't miss it."

"I'll see you there."

She fought the urge to roll her eyes at the two men she loved most in the world. They were one step away from beating on their chests. She glanced at Max. He'd said he loved her. "Daddy, I'm going to make sure he gets home."

With a nod, her father turned on his heel and went to his truck.

Brenda returned to give him instructions on what to do if the burns got worse. After she left, Jackie helped Max down from the ambulance. "Let's get you home."

On the way to his truck, they were stopped by many of the volunteers. It seemed everyone wanted to chat with him like they were longtime friends. She could see the tiredness in his eyes.

With polite smiles she kept moving him closer to his truck. She wanted him alone so they could have that talk. He got in on the passenger side, his eyes heavy.

As she went around to the driver's seat, Adrian stopped her and asked some questions about the white lights she had wanted in the trees surrounding the church. By the time she climbed up into the cab, ready to talk to Max, he'd fallen asleep. His head back and his mouth slightly opened, he looked exhausted. He'd been running since he left for Vegas, then fighting the fire. He had to be wiped out. Well, she'd get him home for now and later they would have that talk. She studied him one more time before turning the key. *God, I love him so much it scares me. Please guide me.*

Could happy-ever-after happen for her?

Chapter Eighteen

The old windows rattled as the north wind tried to get in the church, but the potbellied stove kept everyone warm. Max scanned the room for Jackie. She had to be in the back, helping with the kids. There was standing room only as Pastor Levi opened them in prayer.

Tonight they would be dedicating the building in honor of Cynthia Bergmann and Gabriela Delgado. Their mothers, two women who worked together despite old grudges and family feuds. Their dream was being fulfilled because of Jackie's determination and faith.

Not only had she restored this building, she had given him a new life. For the first time, because of her, he had a place that felt like home. Now, if she said yes, his family would be complete. He hadn't wanted to rush her, but he knew without a doubt what he wanted.

The path God had for them was so clear to him he prayed she saw it, too.

The small troop of miniature angels made their way along the row of windows and down the aisle. Several of the children stopped and waved as they spotted their families.

He saw his brothers searching the room. They saw

Vanessa first and smiled, but Tomas immediately frowned and looked through the crowd. Worry distorted his sweet face.

Max raised his hand to let them know he was there. Isaac nudged his brother. With more enthusiasm than he deserved, the boys waved at him, then went back to being serious angels with a message to deliver. To think he had almost missed this moment.

Shepherds came in from the other door. The angels started singing with so much gusto that their excitement spread through the crowd. "Hark! The Herald Angels Sing" vibrated off the walls.

His throat went dry. Now he was starting to have doubts about the surprise he had planned for Jackie. Pastor Levi had thought it was a good idea, but now he wasn't so sure. He'd never read any of his stuff in public. But his mother and Jackie had encouraged him to write. He wanted to honor the amazing women God had placed in his life. It didn't matter what anyone else thought.

Ethan nudged him on the shoulder. "Hey, you're looking a little pale. You've managed much tougher crowds than this. Anyway, this is for Jackie, and she's going to love it. Girls really like this kind of thing. I'm pretty sure she loves you." He flashed him a cocky grin. "Why, I have no idea, so don't mess it up."

Max put his arm around Ethan. "Thanks." Now he was getting advice from a sixteen-year-old. "You know I'm proud of you, right?"

The teen grinned. "Yeah. I'm kind of proud of you, too. There's Kelsey. I'm going to sit with her to watch the rest of the show. You got this."

Thank You for bringing these boys into my life. He looked back at Tomas and Isaac as they sang with the other angels. Six months ago, he would have said his life was full and he had everything he needed.

He had been clueless about what he was missing.

The double doors at the front of the church opened, and Jackie stood to the side as the kids representing Joseph and Mary entered. The angels started singing "Silent Night," their voices soft this time, as Pastor Levi read the Scripture of the night Christ was born. The pastor's wife, Lorrie Ann, followed that with "Mary, Did You Know?" The older students sang harmony. At that moment, Max knew that he was in the right place and that Jackie was his future.

For the first time, he had something worth fighting for. He might be broken, but God was strong enough to hold him together.

But would Jackie want his broken pieces?

He sang along with the last two songs, never taking his eyes off Jackie. She sparkled under the Christmas lights. When she turned and smiled at him, he felt anything was possible.

The choir all stood together for one last song. One by one, the older kids delivered the gospel, telling of the reason for the Christmas celebration.

Pastor Levi gave a final prayer, then the kids dispersed to join their parents. The boys came running to him. "Did you see us?" Isaac was all grins.

"I did. You sounded great." He kneeled. "Remember you're going to sit with Vanessa for this last part, okay?" They hugged him, then skipped off to sit with their aunt.

Jackie had joined Pastor Levi and was now explaining the history of the church and the reason they were dedicating it to Cynthia Bergmann and Gabriela Delgado, two women who believed the community could come together to heal and celebrate their collective history.

When they finished, the pastor gave Max a nod, and he made his way to the front of the church, past all the people who were such a big part of Jackie. Now they were important to him, because of her.

It was scary to care about other people after so many years of staying detached.

Jackie raised an eyebrow at him, but he just smiled. Once he joined them on the platform, he picked up his guitar and adjusted the strap.

The pastor introduced him. "I think everyone knows Max Delgado, who worked with Jackie and his family to make this night possible. This is just the first of several buildings to get the makeover. Knowing Jackie, by next Christmas we'll have the whole village restored."

Everyone laughed.

The pastor continued. "As we celebrate the birth of Christ, we are reminded of the importance of a mother's love. Jackie and Max both lost their mothers way too early, but they never lost their love. I didn't have the pleasure of meeting Cynthia and Gabriela, but through the Bergmann family and Max, I have grown to know them a little. The love they had for the community and for their families is not gone. It's everywhere around us. Not just in the buildings they wanted to restore, but in their children and even in the grandchildren they'll never meet here on Earth. Max writes music and has written a piece for his mother and for Jackie's. So, as we give thanks for all of God's amazing gifts, we are going to close the night with a remembrance of Cindy Bergmann and Gabby Delgado. And a celebration of families, old and new."

Pastor Levi winked at him, then moved down the steps. "The stage is yours."

Max settled the guitar in his hands, then made the

mistake of glancing at Jackie by his side. Her eyes glistened. Quickly he looked down at the strings.

"Max, what about your hands?" She tilted her head so the crowd wouldn't hear her question.

"I've dealt with much worse pain coming off a bull."

"You're crazy." She leaned in a little closer. "But it makes me very happy that you're writing again. Our mothers would be proud."

With that, she started to follow Pastor Levi down the steps. He reached for her hand and gently tugged her back. "Will you stay with me?"

She nodded. Vanessa and the boys sat in the row behind the Bergmann family.

Sitting with his new friends, Ethan gave him a thumbs-up. This had been his idea when Max came back to the house. Of course, that was before he'd burned his hands.

Our mothers would be proud. The words reverberated around his head. The words he had spent years trying in vain to get from a father who hadn't known how to give.

The emotions that flooded his system nearly choked him. He lowered his head in prayer. He couldn't lose it, not here. Not in front of his brothers. Not in front of all these people.

These people that made up the community he now called home. This was what his mother had wanted for him. It took him a while, but he was here now. And his brothers would grow up surrounded by a family that loved them and supported them.

Taking a deep breath and finding peace in the midst of the turmoil, Max teased a few strings. "In Proverbs, we are told not to forsake our mother's teaching."

His gaze skimmed the crowd and found its way back to Jackie. "Returning to Clear Water has brought me back to the lessons my mother wanted me to learn. Lessons of faith, hope, love and family."

Jackie pressed her lips tight and nodded. Her brilliant eyes shimmered with unshed tears.

His fingers started strumming. The words settled in his brain and merged with the notes.

Everyone faded except for Jackie. He gave her all the words of the love their mothers had for them.

His fingers finally stilled. He had put it all out there: the love, the loss, their mothers' gifts. For a moment the silence was thunderous; then, applause rang as the congregation rose to their feet.

His throat burned. Tomas and Isaac ran up on the stage. Jackie joined them in a big hug. He glanced over her shoulder. All the Bergmann sisters were crying. Even Mr. Bergmann's eyes glistened in the Christmas lights.

Max put his guitar down. Stepping back from her arms, he took her hand. His lungs struggled to take in air.

"Max, that was the most beautiful song I've ever heard."

"You might be a little biased, since it was about our mothers."

"No—" She gasped when he dropped to his knee. Her right hand went to her chest. "Max?"

From inside his jacket, he pulled out the small box Mr. Bergmann had given him. "When I went to talk to your father, he gave me this." He grinned, remembering Mr. Bergmann standing without a word and walking out of the room. Max had panicked, thinking the man was mad. But he had returned, handing him this box. Now Max offered it to Jackie, along with his heart. "This is your mother's ring. When I asked him for his blessing he gave me this. Jacqueline Bergmann, will you do me the honor of being my wife?" His hands shook as he took the ring out of the box and waited.

Her mouth opened, but then closed again.

He broke out into a cold sweat. He squeezed her hand. "I love you, Jackie. With every broken piece of me. It's all yours. I can't imagine any other woman I would want to join our all-boy tribe. Or anyone else who'd be crazy enough to take us."

"I love your all-boy tribe. I love you, Max."

"Is that a yes?"

She nodded. He brought her hand up to his lips and kissed it. He just held her there for a moment before slipping the ring on her finger.

People started clapping and whistling. Max blinked. He had forgotten they weren't alone. Standing, he wrapped his arm around her and pulled her to his side.

The boys jumped around them. "She said yes!"

People started moving around, offering congratulations.

"It's snowing!" someone shouted. Several people rushed to the windows.

Mr. Bergmann frowned. "It's not snowing."

"It is." Nikki stood at the door. "Huge snowflakes."

Danica wrapped herself around her father's arm, as her husband and Adrian followed the others.

Outside, Jackie stayed next to Max, her hand on his arm. Her touch was the only thing keeping him grounded.

Excitement filled the yard as everyone looked at the sky. Huge white flakes already covered the trees and rooftops.

"Max! Look." Tomas turned in a circle with his tongue out.

Max stood on the top step with Jackie. The white Christmas lights illuminated the crystals floating in the air. He laughed.

"Welcome to the Texas Hill Country, Vanessa. I think you and Ethan are the only two snow veterans we have around here."

"Then I'd better get out there and show my nephews how it's done." She scooped up some snow and headed toward Isaac and Tomas. Even the adults were acting like kids.

He and Jackie stood alone.

"Max, look." She pointed to a group of teens. Ethan was showing them how to build a snowman, Kelsey hanging on every word he said.

Jackie tucked her hand under his arm and moved close to him. "There's actually enough snow to do something with. This is amazing."

"Maybe it's a gift from our moms." He leaned his cheek against her head and slipped his uninjured hand over hers.

The laughter and shouts around them faded as he focused on her. She tilted her head back and looked up at him. A snowflake landed on her eyelash. "I'm starting to think you are my gift, Maximiliano Delgado."

"I've been running around like crazy trying to fill the emptiness inside me. Trying to find that boy you believed in. Down deep, I feared he didn't exist." He looked up at the snow falling through the trees, coating the world in a clean blanket of white. "I want to spend all my Christmases with you. You are the Christmas star that led me home. I love you."

"I love you, too. I always have, but I needed to grow up so I could love you the way you deserve. Wholeheartedly and with everything I have. No holding back. Now, are you going to kiss me or not?"

He bent his head and touched his lips briefly to hers. Lifting his head, he grinned at her. "That's all you're getting for now."

A snowball hit him on the shoulder. Danica laughed. "Hey, that's my sister, buddy!"

Max gathered some snow off the bush next to him, forming a ball bigger than his fist. Danica's eyes went wide. "You wouldn't throw that at a pregnant woman!"

Jackie took the ball from him. "He might not, but I will!" The sisters screamed and laughed as they threw snow at each other. The men and children joined in the fun, everyone switching sides when it suited them.

"Max, come on! We need you," Jackie hollered at him.

Taking the steps two at a time he reached for her hand and pulled her back into his arms. Max pressed his lips against Jackie's ear. "Thank you."

"For what?"

"For seeing me. For seeing past the anger and giving me my first Christmas."

She cupped his face. "I'll always see you. You're a good man, Maximiliano, and you deserve to be loved. Together we can make all our Christmas wishes come true."

* * * * *

*If you enjoyed this book, look for the other stories
in the Lone Star Legacy series:*

Texas Daddy
The Texan's Twins

Dear Reader,

Life can take us to places we never planned or imagined. And at times we are unable to get what we think we want, but God has us. He is always there, waiting to heal all hurts.

Jackie and Max's story is a romance, but it is also about relationships with parents, sisters and brothers. Family helps shape who we are—the good, the bad and the painful.

And sometimes the hardest part in life is accepting forgiveness for yourself.

I hope you enjoyed the time with Max and Jackie along with all their siblings. Nikki and Adrian's story is in *Texas Daddy*, and you can find Danica and Reid in *The Texan's Twins*.

I have enjoyed these trips to Clear Water, Texas. Thank you for coming along.

I love chatting with readers. You can find me on Facebook at Jolene Navarro, Author, or drop me a note at Jolene Navarro c/o Love Inspired Books, 195 Broadway, 24th Floor, New York, NY 10007.

Blessings,
Jolene

*When a young Amish woman has amnesia during
the holidays, will a handsome Amish farmer help
her regain her memories?*

Read on for a sneak preview of
Amish Christmas Memories *by Vannetta Chapman,
available December 2018 from Love Inspired.*

"What's your name?"

The woman's eyes widened and her hand shook so that
she could barely hold the mug of tea without spilling it. She
set it carefully on the coffee table. "I don't—I don't know
my name."

"How can you not know your own name?" Caleb asked.
"Do you know where you live?"

"Nein."

"What were you doing out there?"

"Out where?"

"Where was your coat and your *kapp*?"

"Caleb, now's not the time to interrogate the poor girl."
His *mamm* stood and moved beside her on the couch. She
picked up the small book of poetry. "You were carrying this,
when Caleb found you. Do you remember it?"

"I don't. This was mine?"

"Found it in the snow," Caleb said. "Right beside where
you collapsed."

"So it must be mine."

Caleb noticed that the woman's hands trembled as she
opened the cover and stared down at the first page. With one
finger, she traced the handwriting there.

"Rachel. I think my name is Rachel."

Rachel let her fingers brush over the word again and again. Rachel. Yes, that was her name. She was sure of it. She remembered writing it in the front of the book—she'd used a pen that her *mamm* had given her. She could almost picture herself, somewhere else. She could almost see her mother.

"My *mamm* gave me the pen and the book…for my birthday, I think. I wrote my name—wrote it right here."

"Your *mamm*. So you remember her?"

"Praise be to *Gotte*," Caleb's *dat* said, a smile spreading across his face.

"Is there someone we can call? If you remember the name of your bishop…" Caleb had sat down in the rocker his mother had vacated and was staring at her intensely.

They all were.

She closed her eyes, hoping to feel the memory again. She tried to see the room or the house or the people, but the memory had receded as quickly as it had come, leaving her with a pulsing headache.

She struggled to keep the feelings of panic at bay. Her heart was hammering, and her hands were shaking, and she could barely make sense of the questions they were pelting at her.

Who were these people?

Where was she?

Who was she?

She needed to remember what had happened.

She needed to go home.

Don't miss
Amish Christmas Memories *by Vannetta Chapman,*
available December 2018 wherever
Love Inspired® *books and ebooks are sold.*

www.LoveInspired.com